MIA & MICHAEL

By Joseph James

ISBN: 9798374184495

Imprint: Independently Published

Cover design by: Graham Cavendish

For my Husband, who believed in me, who encouraged me to put pen to paper and stood by me.

For my horses, Smokey JOSEPH and Captain JAMES, my motivation and sacrifice.

MIA, 4TH APRIL
11:30PM

For some people the last four hours would have been such a regular occurrence in their lives, almost a non-event. It may have warranted a Facebook status which would soon be forgotten come the morning, or for others probably not even worthy of that. But for me I had just had the most comfortable, yet exciting night of my entire life. Comfortable, yet exciting… now there were two words most people wouldn't put together in a sentence, yet they were two words I had spent a lifetime trying to put together and achieve. Four hours is such a short time, in a lifetime, even with the additional three hours prep I had put myself through before leaving the house, and the dance of butterflies that had made an appearance in my stomach all day before the event. Even with all that, it was still a short time. I should have been ready for sleep from all the overexcitement alone, but I wasn't. Instead I sat on the bottom step of my one bedroomed house in a complete day dream, one shoe on, one shoe off, my handbag abandoned on top of the pile of shoes by the front door, my lipstick lay alone on the carpet when it had fallen along with a load of loose change. I was usually quite house proud, some might say too house proud, but right now I didn't care for tidying up, that could wait for another day. I wanted to enjoy this feeling of happiness, a feeling that had been missing from my life for a long time.

Sitting on my steps my mind played back to the gentle way he had taken hold of my hand as we'd walked onto the escalators that would take us up to the cinema screens. I had always been very conscious of my hands, my first job out of school seeing them endure far too much manual labour for my liking, but there hadn't been many options for me back then. My now regular visit to Amy, my amazing nail lady, had done wonders in improving their look and my confidence about my hands in general was starting to grow as time rolled on. That and my constant moisturising, which was starting to have an impact on maintaining the softness I desired.

Tonight I'd felt like a sixteen-year-old out on a first date. And in some ways, it technically was my first date, which seemed crazy considering I was 34 years old. His long fingers had interlaced with mine, and the little squeeze he'd given me had sent a bolt of lightning through my whole body, the tingling lasting the rest of the date, and they are still bouncing around inside of me right now just remembering. He'd not commented on how my hands matched his size for size, something else I'd spent far too long worrying before meeting him, as I knew mine were big. We'd just looked at each other and smiled that silly smile I'd only ever seen other people give each other. His eyes like deep pools of chocolate brown that I could lose myself in, blocking out the harsh world around us. With only eyes for each other we'd nearly missed the escalator levelling out, we'd both given a nervous giggle as we'd stepped off the grooved metal with a fast-silly walk as our legs tried to get back into a normal pace. We never let go of each other as we made our way over to collect our tickets and as we walked to the popcorn queue, oblivious to everything and everyone around us.

For a first date we hadn't really done much talking. The Film was longer than I'd thought, and when we'd finally got out we'd decided to grab a quick drink in the Weatherspoon's pub within the same complex, neither of us was quite ready to end the night, I know I felt like it had only just begun,   The pub was alive with people enjoying a Friday night out, all buzzing with that end of the week feeling, two days of freedom stretching out in front of them. That thought of no work the next day was beaming across many of the young faces who were pleased to escape the 9-5 that bound their weeks. Drinks were flowing, lads were trying to impress the many beautiful girls with their funny stories, the laughter bringing a life to the place I'd not experienced in a while. I'd only ever been in here early mornings previously for a fry up before work. That was before I worked hard to keep my frame as slim as I could, which was a constant battle and one I'd started to grow used to with the lack of food. I liked it in here by night, which was sad in a way, so many years I'd wasted hiding myself away from the world. The pub was too noisy for any 'get to know you' chats, the usual first date stuff to see if you are compatible, even on the basics. But it didn't matter. I already knew quite a lot about the man holing a pint in his hand, leaning into me to whisper in my ear. We tried to talk about the film, how much we'd both enjoyed it, safe topics, and our first shared experience together. I sipped at my Gin & Tonic, a flavour I was still trying to embrace, my pint days behind me, a lower calorie option stealing its place. Three months of chatting almost daily on the dating site had helped make tonight a bit easier. I knew about his parents, his job, all the usually stuff people might cover about each other on a first date. He knew a lot about me too, but maybe not as much as he should have. That could come later, I didn't want to ruin the moment, the date, or my happiness just yet.

I finally took myself off to bed. I lay down in my comfortable surroundings and admired the room around me. I'd loved decorating this room, making it just how I had always wanted a room to be. I was never able to express myself in my décor until three years ago, when it mattered what impression I gave. This room was my safe place now, where I came to relax and unwind, where I came to be me. Everything around me was a reflection of who I was and what made me who I was. It was more than just colours on a wall, or pictures in a frame thrown together in a rush to get a room done. I had spent ages getting it just right so that I always had one space where everything was alright. But tonight, even my relaxing surrounding weren't working. I was just too happy to sleep. Something I never thought could happen. I closed my eyes to see if that worked, but nothing happened except the image of his face, there, as if he was in the room with me. I wish I could freeze time, freeze this happy moment, to make tonight last forever.

MICHAEL, 6TH
APRIL 10:30AM

As I sat on my sofa looking down at my bulging beer belly I wondered what people actually saw in me. I wondered what I actually saw in myself for that matter, and that was the hardest part. And I wondered why I couldn't make myself happy, no matter how hard I tried. I'd not gone out in two days now, angry at myself for not being on that 'high' other people seemed to achieve so easily, angry with myself for being selfish and not embracing this life I had been given. There were people far worse off than me who seemed to be able to achieve happiness with the cards they had been dealt in life, why couldn't I?

I stood up and made my way to my kitchen. My house and the expensive belongings around me were the only thing I had to show for years of hard work and labour. Four bedrooms, two bathrooms, deep pile carpet throughout, and a garden that required one of those sit on lawn mowers. I was the envy of many of my friends, and family. Not in a jealous way, but in an admiring kind of way that only friends and family seem to share. But still with all that it didn't make me happy on the inside. There was something missing from the house, in my mind it was a bit bland, but no one else seemed to notice that. I held regular parties and hosted many meals for my friends, and they all seemed to love the place and my company and they would all go home happy. I loved cooking for large groups, it gave me a tiny sense of belonging, and a few hours of escape from reality. I could put on being that life and soul of the party I almost believed it myself, but then after the guests had gone and I'd tidied away the mess they had left behind, I was left sat in my beautiful, soulless and very empty house with only the voices in my head for company, and I still felt no real happiness. If anything, these nights brought a deeper loneliness that seemed to take an age to get over.

The latest girl I'd met and taken out, in a line of girls far too long to mention, was beautiful. Absolutely stunning. She really was. Oddly enough her nails had been the first thing to immediately grab my attention when we'd first met. Painted to perfection, the fourth fingernail on each hand had been sprinkled with sparkles that glittered in the night lights. I'd loved the way they looked as I'd taken her hand in mine. I had to force myself to stop looking at them, I didn't want her to think I was being weird or anything. Her hair was perfectly straight, and her makeup applied with a perfection only gained through years sat in front of a mirror practicing. I wanted to make the effort with this one, wanted to make it work, I needed to stop playing the field as it wasn't making me happy, and time was ticking on as my mother would say. I wanted to make this beautiful lady feel special, even if I didn't really feel that way about her, or life, but I could see something in her that I wanted to get to know. I was fed up of trawling the internet to find the perfect soulmate, it was making me feel cheap and desperate. It wasn't the way my parents had met, and it wasn't how I wanted to do things. But I didn't know what I wanted really, and I certainly didn't know how to go about finding it. I struggled with my confidence when I was out socially, struggled to strike up a conversation with women off the cuff, none of it felt natural, even though people would comment on how confident they thought I was. I was good at putting that face on though, they would never know how I was really feeling inside, that game face of mine so well practiced

I could almost believe it myself. Almost. At least sat behind a computer screen I could say the right things, be the person people expected me to be, be the man a woman wanted. I just had to keep that going, now we were on face to face contact and had started the dating process.

She was nice. That was all I could think. Nice. What a weak word, what a weak man I was. She was nice, and she was undoubtedly beautiful, but I had no desire to jump into bed with her, to go beyond holding hands with her, or to even kiss her. I didn't fancy her even though she was beautiful, but I did want to get to know her. I annoyed myself with these mixed emotions, contradicting each other and arguing with one another in my head. With a kiss I could close my eyes and be someone else, yet feel the warmth of another person, for just a moment, maybe that was what I needed, warmth, but more than anything I needed to not mess it up this time. On paper she was perfect. She had an interesting job, we seemed to like the same sort of stuff, she laughed in the right places at things I said, and she looked at me with a passion in her eyes most girls didn't show. There was something deeper with this one, something genuine, like she wanted to really get to know me too, before taking it to the next step. Most girls I'd met weren't like that. She didn't just want me for my money, or the life style I could bring her. She didn't even know I had money, that didn't seem to be what was driving her. I'd tried to look back at her with that same deep longingness, but I dint know if I was carrying it off as well. That deep longing was for something else, something most people just wouldn't understand. I'm not sure if I really understood it myself to be honest. The thoughts I'd managed to keep at bay for years were starting to get stronger and wanted to have poll position in my mind. Those thoughts wanted to be listened too.

There was a loud knock at the door, it snapped me out of my deep thoughts. A moment of panic, what if it was her, I couldn't have her see me like this. Then I remembered, she didn't know my address yet. I slowly stood and made my way to the front door hoping the caller would go away by the time I got to them. They knocked again. I stole a glace through the peephole before pulling down the handle that let the world in. It was my mother.

"Well…" she said, with that expectant look she always gave me before she'd even stepped into the house.

"Come in, I'll put the kettle on mum." I brought myself some time.

Whilst the kettle boiled I busied myself preparing two cups, one with two sugars for her, and mine with an unhealthy three. I plated up some nice biscuits I always kept hidden in the cupboard for such an occasion and placed them on the kitchen table between the two of us. I didn't eat biscuits any other time but there were certain things my mum liked and expected when she visited people. One of them being a biscuit with her coffee, which had to be presented on a plate, and another not being turned away from the door, even if she had arrived for an unannounced visit. It was easier to go with the flow sometimes with her, and not point out that unannounced visits were not always convenient. She had a heart of gold, and a lot of time on her hands, there was no malice in any of her ways, and in all honestly, she wasn't interrupting anything this time.

"Well…" she asked again.

"She was nice mum, I think you'd like her" I smiled and then lifted my cup of coffee to my lips, taking a slow sip.

"Is that all your giving me?!" She punched my arm in the playfulness was she always had. My mum loved her boys, we were her world.

"You know me mum, nice is a big thing. I'm sure you'll get to meet her one day." A line I knew would please her and stop any further digging. It worked.

We spent the next hour sat at my table, had another cup of coffee and a couple of biscuits as I listened to a lot of chat from mum. She updated me on all the family news and events that had taken place in the last week, in great detail! Most of it I already knew, I was close to my brothers and we spoke often, even if just by text. Most of her updates had also been totally embellished, another of my mother's ways. Things snowballed in her mind, and I don't think she even knew she was doing it. There was nothing harmful meant by it, but I knew all the stories had been told to the man at the butchers, the ladies in the bakery and hairdressers, and anyone else in the community who had paused for a moment to talk to her. And each time she stopped and talked, the event, whatever it may be, had grown in my mother's head. It was like she thrived on the drama of it all, it made her feel wanted and needed in the community, it made her feel wanted and needed full stop. It was how she filled her day now we had all long-left home. My father spent most of his time at the sailing club, leaving her at home with nothing to do except clean and reclean their already clean home. I didn't know if he was escaping her, or really liked sailing, but it had always struck me as a little odd, the amount of time he actually spent away from her. But then again, I didn't really know him so well. There was something there, or rather there was something missing between us. We'd had just never really clicked. Our relationship was never nasty, but never easy either. We almost avoided each other if we could help it. Maybe he could see the real me and didn't like what he saw.

MIA, 12TH MAY
8.30PM

It was date night again, and as I sat across the table from him on our third meet up a ball of nerves had joined me again for the evening. Date number two had gone well, though I had played it safe and chickened out and had opted to go to the cinema again. We'd had a nice time and had gone for a drink after the film again. And he hadn't pushed for anything more. But I realised I'd have to give in and go for a 'face on' date if we were to make it much further than date number two. Men wanted more than just to sit next to someone in a cinema screen both facing the same way, not looking at each other, I knew that. They could do that with their mates after all, or even on their own. I was being silly really, as this lovely man I was fast growing attached to did nothing to make me feel uncomfortable, or to warrant the volume of nerves anything above excitement. When I was behind a computer screen and talking to him online I could be anyone, and be brave, but here, in the restaurant, with him sat 3 feet in front of me, I could only be me. I just hoped he like the real me. I wasn't ready for the bubble to burst just yet.

I'd suggested a Chinese, which had gone down well. Not only was it one of my favourite cuisines, but a few years ago I had made it a mission of mine to learn to eat with chopsticks. I'd picked it up surprisingly quickly, my hands adapting to the delicate operation far better than the day job they were having to do at the time. It had also been something positive to focus on when everything else around me got tuned upside down, something that took my mind off things, even if just for a moment in time here and there. There had been many reasons I'd wanted to learn, one of them reasons was an influence on today's restaurant choice, and another, the ability to use them properly never failed to impress others. I'd noticed people always watched the tips of the chopsticks when other people ate using them, waiting for food to be dropped or pinged off as the two ends of the chopsticks often slid over each other from lack of coordination. They watched the ends, never the hands, and for this first meal out together, I didn't want him looking at my hands. He'd held them on more than one occasion but looking at them made me very self-conscious.

I ordered soup for starters and a prawn Chow Mein for my main. Two options I knew I could carry off 'dainty' with confidence. I don't know why I worried so much. He ordered ribs, a very hands-on starter which always required complete attention from the consumer, followed by beef Chow Mein. This would have been my second choice, but I didn't want to risk chewy beef, I wanted something that required little chewing, easy to swallow without having to be too 'eaty'. I knew no one would understand if I tried to explain what I meant by that, so I'd never bothered explaining it to anyone. I'd never had reason of late to explain it. It was a thought that just stayed in my head. My mother had thought I was a picky eater all my life, but that had turned out to be the least of her worries.

Our food choices worked well for me. We chatted away like a proper couple catching up on their day, his eyes meeting mine long enough to stay engaged in what I was saying, and to let me know he was listening, but then the succulent meat on the bone in front of him requiring his attention and drawing his eyes back down to his plate. The conversation flowed easily, and I had such a buzz I was struggling not to over smile. Never attractive. We picked up from a chat we had been having on line this week about his work. He had a busy job which often kept him working long hours, hence this being only the third time we had physically met face to face, but we were talking on line most days now, which had been nice. I didn't mind right now about him working so much, and I didn't think I would mind anyway. I'd gotten use to spending a lot of time on my own, even though I had a large circle of friends, who more often than not were 'busy' these days. My mind wondered back to a time in the distance past as he worked on getting the last bit of meat off the bone in front of me. I remembered even in a crowd I never felt like I was in the same room as everyone else, never felt I was totally getting the vibe of whatever we were all doing. I couldn't put my finger on it for a long while. The feeling I remember the most vividly though was the feeling of loneliness, even when I was surrounded by others who would claim I was their good friend. Though none of my friends knew it, or remotely even picked up on it, I had been good at putting that right face on at the right time. I presume they all thought I was having a jolly good time, wherever we were. Talking about feelings had not been on the top of my friends' agendas. On the face of it, if they managed to get me out somewhere I was the life and soul of the party, way too over the top to the point of being false, though they never saw that, too drunk to realise what was right in front of them. I always had to be the loudest, the funniest, the one everyone wanted to talk to and be with, but inside I was as hollow as an Easter egg. I wasn't being the real me, and I couldn't be the real me for fear of losing my friends. I lost them anyway, in the end, a lot of them gave up asking me out. They got fed up with the feeble excuses I kept coming up with when I got tired of playing the part they all seemed to love me for. House visits for a cosy chat weren't on the offer back then either, they only wanted me as their show piece and not a lot else.

'Mia… am I boring you, sorry' he spoke softly, bringing me back into the room, a room I very much felt part of and wanted to be in. I pushed the memory back to that dark corner it had sprung from.

'Oh sorry' I stalled for time, not wishing to share the memory with anyone, let alone him. 'I was just thinking how nice and relaxed this is. It's like I've known you ages.' I smiled, a twinkle to me eye bringing a smile to his face. It made me tingle inside, his smile.

'Here..' he quickly wiped his fingers on the napkin on his lap and offered his hand to me across the table. I took it, the embrace making me feel warm inside, wanted, our eyes losing the rest of the room as they locked in a deep passion that I could feel oozing from us both. When I had feelings like this I could pretend it would all be ok. That I was normal.

At the end of the night there was no pressure for anything, just a gentle hand hold as we stood outside the restaurant waiting for my taxi to arrive. He'd made it really easy for me and ordered two taxi's, one for me and the second one for him. We wouldn't have that awkward 'do you want to come in' conversation as the taxi dropped me off, we could leave the night here, at the curb as we went our separate ways. It was a relief in one way, but part of me didn't want that either, didn't want the night to end, to have days between the next time I would get to see him. Dating was making me feel alive, liked, part of the world again. It was like a drug I couldn't get enough of. You know you have to stop, or in my case tell the truth, but you just can't, you just want that one more go before you have to face the truth.

MICHAEL, 13TH MAY 12:30AM

I'd just got in from another 'successful' date, if you could call it that. It had ticked all the right boxes for a successful date, if you were watching us from afar that is. But there was one box it wasn't ticking for me, but I sort of couldn't put my finger on what it was, and I sort of could but didn't want to admit it and the reason why boxes weren't being ticked, again. It was a difficult thought to process, and it wasn't something I could contemplate saying out loud. It scared me it being in my head.

I sat down at my dining table, large enough to seat ten people, if you sat close enough together, eight people comfortably, and poured myself a Baileys over ice. A Baileys nightcap was fast becoming a bad habit of mine. I'd try and break the cycle tomorrow I told myself, but I needed it right now, just to settle myself. It was another of those lonely nights in my large empty house, and I needed to stop my brain thinking. I rested my head on the table and closed my eyes, ran through the evening step by step in my head. I wasn't ready to go to bed, even though I had told her I was tired, but I'd really needed a bit of space to myself to think, to really work stuff out. Was what I was really feeling a real feeling? I got my phone out and began to google the question, just to see if anyone else had asked the same question. To see if there was anyone else who felt the same.

She was everything a man could want from a woman. So pretty, in a classic way, charming, easy going and she really looked after herself. Again, I'd noted how beautiful her nails were tonight, and her perfect makeup too. Not too heavily applied, but enough to enhance her features and bring a brightness to her face that people who didn't wear makeup often lacked, in my unknowledgeable opinion. But she wasn't over the top girly, in that childish way many of the woman I had dated before often were. One previous girlfriend sprung to mind who I should never have dated full stop, a mistake that was hard to forget. I pushed her away and thought about tonight. The woman I had taken out was funny, interesting, and completely held my attention. It really felt like I could be best friends with her one day, that I could confide all my deepest secrets to her and yet have a laugh at the same time as only best friends can. Only women don't want male best friends, unless they are gay, or that's what I thought anyway. They want someone to love them, romance them, and look after them, have babies with them and settle down with them. I could do two out of the five, time would tell if that would be enough to keep her interest.

I took a large mouthful of the cooled Baileys, letting it slide down the back of my throat. My mind drifted back to memories from secondary school. It hadn't been the easiest of times, but then again, I hadn't met a single person who'd had an easy ride at school for one reason or another. They say, 'it makes you the person you are today,' but I've never really got that statement. I've never knew who 'they' were either... did 'they' actually exists? Or was it one of those stories passed along through the generations, each person saying it to convince themselves that school was okay in the end and they were normal after all. Everyone just wanted to be normal and like everyone else. Maybe it did make me who I am today, but I wasn't convinced. I think it just taught me how to pretend to be who people wanted me to be, the person they see before them today. Basically, I think it taught me how to pretend to fit in. Drama had been the only reason I got out of bed some days and made the five-mile bus journey in to school. The journey alone was tortuous with kids bullying other kids, bus drivers shouting at kids to sit down, and just the general mayhem of a public bus swamped with school kids of all ages. I felt for any regular paying customers as it must have been a horrid experience for them. But Drama took me away from all of that, it took me to another place, to somewhere I could be whoever I wanted to be, or to whoever the teacher had told me to be for the play or scene we were working on at the time. I just liked the idea of being someone else, someone who was not me. Someone who really knew who they were in life. And for some strange reason I'd had a flare for it. It was a shame I'd given it up really, but my father never really approved, and when it had come to careers talks at the school, he had made it known that no offspring of his was going to take Drama beyond the compulsory years, it was not an option for me for my GCSE's. At the time it was like my only escape had been cruelly ripped away from me and blocked off. I had been inconsolable for days. But my mother never backed me up or talked my father round to the idea. What he said went, end of, no argument. He was very much the man of the house, and in his eyes, he was teaching us kids how to be the men of the future. That was his contribution to our upbringing, and that was where his contribution had ended.

I took another mouthful of my drink and pushed my chair back, as I forced the memory of my misspent youth away. I put my phone back in my pocket, not wanting to see what my search engine had found for me, the memories in my head enough pain for one night. That regret for my childhood wasn't going to do me any good now, I couldn't change it or wind the clock back, and start over again, and regretting wasn't going to get me through the rest of my life, like 'they' all thought it would.

I laid down in my bed, looked around at the large airy room around me, the stuff of show homes, but I wasn't sure it was me. I forced my eyes closed and let the alcohol take me off to sleep, a sleep I hoped would be void of dreams. Dreams can give you a glimmer of truth, a void would let me rest from thinking so I might then be able to fight on for another day.

OLIVER

My head felt like it was covered in water, like when you are at the swimming pool and you dive to the bottom to see how long you could stay there, everything always sounded muffled around you until you come out of the water again. I could hear sounds around me, but everyone sounded far away, and I felt like I was floating away from everything around me. I liked the swimming pool, but I didn't like this feeling at all, and I didn't know how to make it stop. It didn't feel real, none of it, and I wanted it all to go away. I wanted it to be yesterday again when everything was normal, when I didn't care about much because I didn't need to care about much. Mum always sorted everything out for me, she always cooked me dinners, and got me to school and my friends' houses. She always seemed busy making sure I was happy. And me and dad would go out to places and have fun. He was busy at work a lot mum said, but he always did nice stuff with me. School was okay too, I quite liked it, I got to see my friends and hang out. No one picked on me because my dad didn't live with me, I thought they might, but lots of other people's dads didn't live with them either. And I liked my teacher this year. I heard my friends moaning about things, but I didn't have anything to moan about I didn't think. Everything was nice… yesterday.

Mum had sat me down on the sofa. She looked sort of funny, like she was nervous about something, or angry, but I didn't think I had done anything wrong to be told off. I wondered if she had done something wrong maybe? She started telling me how much she loved me, and how she would always be there for me no matter what, and that I never need to feel alone, it was all a bit weird and I didn't really like it, she was scaring me a bit. I didn't feel alone so why would she say these things. Then she told me. She told me that my dad had died. I didn't really get it at first, I don't think I wanted to get it. Then mum reminded me about my pet rabbit Harry that had gone to heaven. That was last year, but he was old for a rabbit mum had said at the time. And that is where my dad has gone, to heaven. I didn't think he was old enough to go to heaven yet. I thought only old people and old pets went to heaven. But mum explained that sometimes young people went to heaven too. She told me my dad had been poorly, but he never looked poorly to me, and I had only seen him last week. He never told me he was poorly then, but mum said that was because he didn't want me to worry about him. He had told me other stuff before, ages ago, and he had cried, I remember. I didn't understand why he never told me he was poorly, seeing as he had told me other sad stuff. He never said goodbye properly, if he knew he was poorly why didn't he say goodbye?

That was yesterday. I didn't really sleep last night and I'm really tired now, but I still can't sleep, my mind is bouncing about all over the place. Mum let me stay off school today. I wish I had gone to school though so I could have seen my friends, maybe to talk to them about this, maybe to forget what mum had told me. I didn't know, but I needed my mates right now. Mum stayed off work to be with me, but I sort of feel angry with her, and her fussing is starting to annoy me. I know she is trying to be nice, but she just keeps talking, and asking me if I am OK. I wish she would stop. I need to think.

'When will dad have a funeral?' I ask, causing her to stop speaking suddenly.

'How do you know about funerals?' She asks me. She always did that, answer my question with another question.

'Ben at work, his nan died, he told me all about the funeral. And Sam, his grandad died and he went to a funeral. Its where you go to say goodbye. When will I get to say goodbye to dad?'

'I don't know yet Oliver. Its early days, that wouldn't have been sorted out yet.' She only used my full name when she was angry with me, I wasn't sure what she had to be angry about, it was me who's dad had died, not her.

'OK. But I want to go, mum.' She didn't reply, she just looked at me, I couldn't work out what she was thinking, I was usually quite good at knowing what she was thinking, or what mood she was in, but today, I just couldn't tell. I felt so alone.

I wanted it to be yesterday, when I still had a dad.

MICHAEL, 23RD JUNE 6PM

B aileys night had had a good effect in some ways and had kicked me in to touch a bit. I'd not had a drink at home on my own since that night, in fact I'd poured all the alcohol in my house down the kitchen sink in an effort to remove the temptation from my life. Relying on the stuff to sleep was a slippery slope, and I had enough problems to deal with in my head without that in the equation. I didn't need additional issues to resolve right now. It had been tough literally pouring money down the drain, but weirdly satisfying at the same time. The power of taking control. Plus I didn't really care about money at the moment, feeling in control was worth far more to me, and something money couldn't buy anyway. I'd been so gripped with a fear that all I was going to amount to was some sad alcoholic with no real sense of anything, all because I couldn't face up to the truth. I still drank though, just not on my own. When I'd gone to my parents for dinner the other night I'd had a bottle of wine to myself, much to my father's disappointment. He's wanted me to drink ale, beer, a man's drink, like we'd always done, but I was fast going off the taste. I'd also shared several bottles of wine on the couple of dates I'd been on with her, my new woman. Which had been absolutely lovely. Two friends sharing a drink and a giggle. I just didn't want to drink when I got home, when I closed the door to the world, when it was just me and the bottle. That was the key. My thoughts had gone to deep dark places and I didn't want drink making it any worse than it already was for me. Drinking on my own was not doing me any good. I'd thought it was a 'phase' but thinking back about it had made me realise I'd been stuck in this phase, or whatever it was, for a long while now. In fact, I'd always felt like this, and that was a hard thing to admit to yourself. Still, I had my new friend, and she really was helping me, even if she didn't know just how much.

I thought back to our last date, where we'd been out for lunch in the town centre, and then we'd taken a leisurely walk down through Campbell Park. I loved that about my home town. Everything you could want to entertain you was right on your door step, yet just as quick you could be in a peaceful country setting. There were even sheep out grazing on our walk, and we'd not even had to move the car and drive out to the countryside. The main shops were only yards away, yet sheep nibbling grass enjoying a bit of sun on their backs only ten minutes' walk away. A sense of lightness had come over me, the feeling of stresses leaving my body, just for a short moment. I almost had a skip in my step I'd felt that happy. There was no pressure to be anyone or anything as we'd walked hand in hand through the park. We were normal people, just like the people running through the park, just like the other couple we saw holding hands and chatting away. Normal. A world apart from how I felt on the inside, but you had to take those normal feelings when they hit you, that's what would get me though life, or so I thought.

I really liked her because there was no pressure from her. I hated the pressure to behave a certain way that many people put upon you. It helped me emotionally that she was happy with me just holding her hand, never pushing for anything more. We'd had a kiss or two, but it never felt right, not for me anyway. I'd not asked her how she felt, as that would just be weird, and could open up a can of worms that I'd not be able to close the lid back on. But she never pushed for more than a kiss, which I didn't mind, so maybe she felt the same as me. Her hands had not strayed south at all, not like many of the girls I had dated, and she'd not unbuttoned anything that shouldn't be unbuttoned. That was always a massive turn off for me, even if my body was saying something else to them. When that had happened in the past it was often a deal breaker for me, the poor girl not knowing what she had done wrong, but that would often be the last time I saw them.

So, we have another date coming up tomorrow night, and I'd said that I would pick her up from her house. Up to now we'd always met at the place we were going, which made the end of the evening goodbye bit much easier in my mind. I'd pick my friends up, or rather I use to offer to pick them up when we were all still friends, so it slipped out so easily when I'd offered, and once out there I couldn't take it back. That would have looked rude. But it had left me in a state of panic ever since the words had tumbled out, and that was putting it mildly. What if she thought this meant I wanted to stay the night. We'd not talked about that stage of our relationship, and she didn't seem like that kind of girl to just want to jump into bed… but what if… what would I do… I just didn't think I could go through with it again. I'd end up leaving, and then she wouldn't want to be friends anymore. I headed to my drinks cabinet in auto drive, opened the wooden doors only to remember that all the drink had gone, down the sink, there was nothing left. It was probably for the best, but I was left pacing the room, forced into thinking about why I felt like this anyway, rather than blocking it out with the comfort of alcohol.

An hour later, and with a thumping headache I popped two paracetamol in my mouth and swallowed them down with a glass of water. I'd realised I'd have to perform. I'd have to do something my body could easily do, even if my mind wasn't in the same room. And the reason.... I'd done it before, so I knew I could, only this time I'd not run away after, I'd not change my phone number, I'd not be a complete dick about it all. I couldn't. Those days had to stop. This cycle I was trapped in had to stop, and this might be my last opportunity. It was the thought that scared me, but not as much as the truth did.

MIA, 24TH JUNE 7AM

I'd woken early which was a surprise, considering the time I'd finally gone to bed. It had probably been the worst date with him so far, but not because I hadn't enjoyed his company, as I really had. As I lay staring up at my celling I couldn't help but hide the disappointment I felt with myself, at myself, and it was eating me up. Two tears simultaneously left my eyes, one from each eye, symmetrically meandered their way down my face, landing on my pillow either side of my face, so synchronised and perfect in performing their own little dance. I replayed the evening back to myself, something I'd done a lot of lately, only this wasn't a play back I really wanted to see. We'd gone out for a lovely meal in a buzzing restaurant in the main town centre. There had been so many people out enjoying themselves on a sunny evening, it had given the whole place such a lovely vibe and had given me such a lovely happy feeling too. I'd felt on top form, and the most comfortable I'd felt in a long while. Everyone in the restaurant was chatting, the noise building and growing as the night had progressed. But that noise had given us our own little bubble in a funny way, almost hidden from the world in a crowded room. The people around us so engrossed in their own conversations, and trying to be heard by their friends, that no one paid any attention to us, we were just any other couple out on a date minding our own business. I surprised myself how relaxed I'd felt eating in front of him, I'd not worried about my hands once all night, almost forgetting they were an issue for me when I'd first met him. We'd laughed and joked the night away, it felt like I had always known him. I hadn't wanted the waiter to come and collect our desert plates, and I hadn't wanted him to ask for the bill, as that meant it was neatly time to go home, and for the date to be over.

He'd held my hand with the tenderness I was getting use to as we'd walked out of the restaurant and made our way to his car. He'd offered to drive last night and had come and picked me up, something about an early start today prompting the offer I think. It had been the first time he had seen my house, and it has been the first time we had travelled to a date together in the same car. This was a big step for me in my world, where I had been hidden away for so many years. I'd spent all day getting myself ready, and getting my house ready too, just in case he came in after.

Whenever he took my hand in his it sent a wave of excitement through me. It had been like that since our first date. I'd wondered if that feeling would ever became normal, did people stop getting excited about their hand being held? I'd never been with anyone long enough to find that out before, and before that I'd never been with anyone that gave me any kind of excitement when I held their hand, so I just didn't know. I hoped this might be the time that meant I could put all that past stuff behind me once and for all.

I closed my eyes, dreading my mind playing back the next bit of the night. The bit where he pulled up outside my tiny house with its neat front garden. The bit where he placed his hands on top of mine in a romantic embrace, the bit where he leaned forward over the gearstick and handbrake like we were 18-years olds again and kissed my lips so tenderly, unlike an 18 year old might. His hand has risen off mine and gently made its way to my breast. I'd never been touched like that before, and I didn't know what to do, I didn't know how to be, how to respond. I froze, taking a short sharp breath in as his hand caught my nipple. I heard a little sound leave my mouth, one I'd not heard from myself before. To me it was the sound of shear panic. To him I think it was the sound of a woman being turned on. Maybe I was. I didn't know. At the same time, he was trying to encourage my hand along the inside of his leg towards his growing groin. And that's where it all went wrong. I pulled back from the kiss, thanked him for a lovely evening as I scrabbled for the door handle in the unfamiliar car and got out as quickly as I could.

"Bye" I'd leant back inside the car from the safe distance of the passenger side, "See you soon, hope it goes okay tomorrow." I called as I slammed the door with far more force than was necessary. Sometimes I didn't know my own strength. I walked the short distance to my front door, fumbling in my handbag with my back to him whilst trying to locate my front door key, almost dropping the rest of the contents of my bag all over the path. I could still hear his car ticking over behind me. I wanted him to drive off, go, and at the same time I want to turn around and invite him in for coffee. That's what normal people did, especially at my age. I'd behaved like some silly teenager and I was so pissed off with myself. It was all happening so quick, and I'd just buried my head in the sand like I had done on so many occasions for so many years. Rather than talking to this kind man who I thought so much of, and who had just brought me dinner, I'd behaved appallingly, and I knew it. If nothing else I had been completely rude to a friend, and I had been raised better than that. I just hoped that I would be given the chance to explain it to him, maybe even to make it up to him. That didn't even make sense to me, how was it ever going to make sense to him. Given that both my parents no longer spoke to me, my own flesh and blood, I didn't hold out much hope for anyone else in the world, and I'd just pushed away the one friend I had last night. I rolled over onto my side, and brought my knees up to my chest, like I had on done so many occasions before, my childhood comfort position. The tears weren't so slow and meandering now, they were falling with the force of an angry waterfall.

An hour later I'd finally stopped crying. My body and mind felt totally exhausted from the effort of crying, let alone the stress and reason behind the tears. Even so, sleep wasn't an option for me, I know that relief wouldn't happen so I forced myself up out of bed, and told myself I just needed to get on with the long day ahead of me. I'd managed to come through worse mental torture before, I could do this, with a bit of effort.

MIA, 24TH JUNE 8PM

I was right, it had been a long day, trying to fill the time, whist trying not to look at my phone. It was even worse than a day at work. At least that offered some distraction. I'd even taken to hiding the dam phone in the draw at one point, just so I wasn't staring aimlessly at the unlit screen. I'd cleaned the house, changed my bedding, and done some online banking that was a little over due, all of which didn't take too long to complete. I was left thinking of things to do. I'd tried to do some gardening, hoping the fresh air would help but my heart just wasn't in it, and now I was sat on the sofa with the TV on trying to keep my mind off all sorts of stuff. Jeremy Kyle's Show was on, it made me feel a little more normal, mentally normal, but I'm sure he'd still have a field day with me if I was sat on his stage. I didn't get why people aired their woes in front of millions of people and a judgemental live audience. The thought of the public rejection alone put me right off using that as a possible route for talking about things.

I looked at my phone, again, and wondered if it was broken. I turned it off, waited a minute, then turned it back on again. Still noting. My logical sensible head said he was just busy, after all he had told me that today was an early start and a long day, just because mine wasn't not everyone had been filling time. But my emotional head, the one that seemed to rule me more and more these day was telling me I had blown it last night and that I wouldn't be hearing from him again any time soon.

I don't know why I did it, but my hand moved to the one little space in my house where I kept the old me tucked away. It was a hidden space in a little draw in a unit that was sat under the stairs. I don't even know why I kept any of that stuff, I had moved on, was a new me, and that is what I had fought so hard for, and had spent so much money on to achieve. I couldn't stop myself from looking though. My hand pulled the draw open, and I took out the small pile of papers. I held them in front of me, the TV now just a slight background noise. The first bit of paper was an internet printout of the sale of my old house. I'd brought at the right time and made a good amount of money from the sale, money that had been a great help. I looked around my humble abode that I was sat in now, small, compact, but home. I was also now nicely mortgage free courtesy of this bit of paper finding a nice cash buyer for my old house. A mortgage was not a stress I'd needed at the time or even now. And that freedom wasn't the only thing my big house had had paid for. My mother had not been able to hide her disappointment when I told her I was selling up and downsizing. It had been the final straw for her, no going back. Disappointment didn't come close to how she reacted to that news. I was the one she told all her friends about; I was her success story. To take that away from her was to rip the soul from our relationship. And it had. The whole thing had.

The letter heading for the next bit of paper stuck out above the sales literature paper. I could see the distinctive NHS logo, and hospital address underneath. I didn't even need to read the actual letter; the flash back was there instantly. The numerous trips to that building, I knew its rabbit warren corridors inside out and back to front. A building that had changed my life forever, for the better, but a building that also caused me pain like I'd never known before. I didn't think it was a good idea, especially in my current state to carry on looking through these memories, it was all still too raw. I put the pile of papers back in the hidden draw, my eyes closed as I slide the draw back in place, forcing the memories in my mind back into a dark corner at the same time.

Just at that moment my phone lit up. A text from him. I held the phone in my hand, enjoying the way his name looked upon my screen, pausing, not wanting to open the text just yet. Whilst it sat unread there was still hope. Hope was good.

MICHAEL, 30TH JUNE 6PM

I was on my way to pick her up for a drink, I'd not seen her since last week, and in a funny way I was missing her. I'd kept to texting all week though, not being able to face an actual phone call, but it had been comforting having her there at the end of a message, someone who wanted to listen, someone who would respond, and understand when I said I'd had a rubbish day at work. That was an easy lie to carry off over a text, work wasn't really the issue, but I'd had many bad days this week none the less, I just didn't want to tell her what was really making them bad. Not yet anyway.

I nervously clicked on the indicator and turned my car into her road. I pulled up and beeped. Rude I thought but it kept the hellos nice and easy as she got into the car. I didn't want to walk up to her door, and risk being invited in before we went out, I wanted the safety of a crowded room when we got chatting. How could I be so messed up I asked myself as she leant across and gave me a peck on the cheek before clicking her seatbelt on.

"That was a nice hello" I said as I pulled away and drove out of her street, even that sounded silly and pointless out loud.

"Thanks" was all she could muster. Then a few moments awkward silence followed. They felt like a life time.

"So, how's your week been?" she asked after a few minutes,

breaking that silence and stopping the tumble weed from gathering momentum.

"Busy at work, but OK, you know how it goes." Was all I could offer, but it was enough to get the conversation stared, and then it started to flow a little more normally. By the time we reached the restaurant things were back to how they were a week ago. Easy. On the outside.

We took our seats as directed by Jamie, our waiter for the evening. He seated us at a cosy table for two in the far corner of the restaurant and handed us the menu and the drinks list, running through the specials on offer today before leaving us to decide. The candle light reflected and bounced off the glass walls that surrounded this section of the seating area. It had 'romance' and 'love' written all over it. It should have been perfect, but my nerves had kicked in. I wasn't being honest to myself, or this kind lady sat in front of me, but wheels were spinning that I didn't know how to stop. And even if they did stop, I didn't know what to do to fix the mess they would leave behind. Maybe I needed to see a doctor I thought to myself. Maybe I was depressed. Maybe that's what it was.

The waiter was a bit over keen for my liking, almost trying to ensure a good tip was given in his direction. I just wanted him to stop fussing, let me read the menu and choose my drink, I just wanted him to go away and give us some space. To be fair he was just trying to do his job, and increase his low wage, who could blame him, and he did recommend a good wine which I pretended I didn't know about, so I ordered a bottle. It seemed lying to those around me was getting to be a life habit of mine. He swiftly returned with the recommended wine, all proud looking, and poured us both a large glass, "just the one then" I said to her as he finally left us alone. I gave her the best smile I could as we clinked glassed and took a sip of wine. Well, mine was more of a gulp, but I don't think she saw that bit. I hadn't ordered myself a soft drink to go with my wine, something I would always do when I drove, but something had clicked inside me when we sat down, and I had every intention of getting thoroughly pissed and leaving the car at the restaurant. I needed a blow out, before I blew.

We worked our way through the evening, small chat was easy and filled the time, we had a laugh, and ate some very nice food. From the outside looking in we'd had the perfect evening, and in many ways we had. Looking at it from the inside we had had a nice time too, I'd even managed to forget about other stuff for a bit. The laughing, and the alcohol, both kicking in, made it easy to pretend everything was alright and normal. That was the bit that was bugging me. I got on with her so well, and we had such a good laugh together. Once we got going, nothing was difficult about spending time in each other's company. She had an amazing outlook on life, and seemed so confident in herself but not in an arrogant way. She was such a positive person to be around, you couldn't help but feel inspired and happy around her, and she really looked after herself too. I wasn't sure why, but this was a big thing for me, women who looked after themselves, and made the effort. But it was never for sexual reasons, it didn't turn me on like that. It mattered that she kept her nails well, and her makeup was immaculate, and it mattered that her hair had some length to it and was beautiful. I hated to see long hair scooped up into a tight ponytail, pulling a beautiful face into a startled look. Unless someone was exercising of course, but other than that I saw it as a waste of femininity. Was this what men went for, was that how other men thought, was that what other men fell for? Was this falling in love? I just didn't know the answers to any of those questions, as behind the laugher, and the drinking, and the joking about, when I closed my door on the world, I didn't know if I was falling in love, or what falling in love was, and to be honest it scared me. My head was filled with so much other stuff, weird thoughts that were getting harder and harder to push away to the back of my mind. Was it 'falling' if I had those thoughts? It was a question I just couldn't answer myself, and I didn't know who could help me answer that question. I was beginning to think that I might need help to answer that question, but right now, I didn't care as I'd had the best night I'd had all week, and the wine was well and truly kicking in. I just needed to enjoy a moments relief, a moment to feel lightheaded without a care in the world. Tonight, I would go with the flow, let happen what might happen, and worry about the rest in the morning. One last test for myself.

MICHAEL, 1ST JULY 7AM

I was awake, but I didn't want to open my eyes, that would make it all too real. I knew I was not in my own bed, and I wasn't sure if I was going to throw up. The covers resting against my face didn't smell like my own 'blue sky's' that I insisted on using, and the covers didn't have the same crisp feel that mine had. I was a bit particular about my bedding, I liked to feel like I was at a hotel with crisp ironed fresh sheets encasing me each night. It created a lot of washing and ironing for me but that was how I liked it. The other big give away that I wasn't at home was the curled up warm body I could feel next to mine, its heat radiating towards me, making me feel a tad too hot, and a bit claustrophobic. One foot was hooked over mine too, in a fond way only regular bed partners seem to fit and mould together. Only this wasn't regular for me, and I wanted to leap up and run out of the house and back to the place where I could bury my head in the sand.

"Morning sleepy head" I heard her voice, all soft next to me, trying to rouse me from my non-sleep. I'd been pretending, again, whilst I tried to piece together the events of the previous evening. Events that had led to me waking up in a bed that wasn't my own! I didn't like what my memory was presenting to me right now. The drink, it was the drink that had done it. I'd let my guard down, the alcohol helping me block out my real desire. Whatever was going on inside with me my body still had external needs I guessed.

"That was a surprise, last night… a nice one though" she whispered in my ear as she ran her delicate fingers up the inside of my leg, stopping just short of my penis, waiting for a signal from me that we were going to repeat the previous night's encounter all over again. I didn't want to crush her feelings right now, but I felt so vulnerable, all naked and exposed in her arms. And I did like her, but I just couldn't have sex again, right now, with her, a woman, sober. My body had had its fix, even if my mind didn't like it, and that sounded selfish to all parties, including me. I'd need the influence of alcohol to even remotely go there at this moment in time, and I realised that made me sound like a right bastard. Not a thought I liked about myself.

I rolled onto my side, her hand almost becoming trapped between my thighs. This was good, she couldn't now easily progress her hand along its intended route. Her hair had fallen over her face in a wispy fashion. She had a nice morning look, a strange mix of seductive, and content. I'd seen a lot worse in my time, I just wish it was a look I could fall in love with and a look I wanted to make love to. I didn't understand what I meant by that, that lack of understanding becoming a common theme in my head. Or maybe I did understand, and that was what was scaring me. I kissed her gently on the mouth, my eyes closed for a moment, waiting for that signal from my body. It didn't arrive. I knew it wouldn't.

"I'd love to stay in bed with you all morning, you know that, but I've got to get going" I started to gently prize myself out of the entanglement I found myself in.

"So soon?" Her face looked a little hurt, confused perhaps. I could see her questioning herself, asking if she had done something wrong last night.

"I'm so sorry" I kissed her again, stalling for time, thinking up that plausible excuse that would get me out of the house without causing pain. "My mum wants me to take her out to see her sisters, she doesn't drive anymore, and I've been promising her for weeks I'd take her." I was pretty sure ladies like men who cared about their mothers and would therefore be happy letting me leave the bed without making me feel any worse than I already did.

"I could come too..." She left the statement hanging in the air as she looked at me hopefully, longingly, willing me to say yes.

"I'm sorry" A word that I just seemed to keep repeating itself from me lately. "I think my mum wants me all to herself, you know. A certain lady has been taking up a lot of my time lately, and I think it's just taking my mum a bit of time to get use to sharing me." I was proud of my quick thinking, even if it made me sound wishy washy and like a mummy's boy. But her eyes softened and she gently released her grip on me, I knew she had swallowed the lie right down to the depths of her heart.

"I understand that." She kissed me again. "I'd love to meet her one day though."

"One day." I replied, with a return kiss to her. None of it I wanted, and I knew it would never actually happen if I had anything to do with it, but this seemed the easiest way out of the situation I found myself in without casing too much stress and upset.

Half an hour later I found myself sat in the local coffee house staring into my Latte, hoping the answer would appear in the milky froth beneath me. I liked it in here. It was a small independent coffee house where I could come and just be me. It was always busy enough, but not in a stressful way like some of the main high street coffee houses were. It suited me anyway. I liked to be with people, but not to be swamped by people, all talking loudly to make themselves looked important. In this quirky backstreet coffee house, I could sit down, enjoy my coffee and relax. You could sit for as long as you like with the same cup of coffee here, they didn't mind, and I had done just that on more than one occasion, losing track of time more than anything as my mind worked overtime, options toing and froing in my head. They did make delicious sandwiches here, and if I was passing at a lunch time I'd often drop in, the place was a win win. But right now I couldn't face food, I just needed some caffeine to kick start my day, and I needed the head space this gem of a little place offered me, before I went home, before I faced the world, before I faced my mind.

MIA, 1ST JULY 9AM

I was still in bed at 9am which was very unlike me. I was the sort of person who liked to get up early and make the most of the day. But this morning I was happy to lay in my bed and take a bit of time for myself, waking at a slow pace. The window was open, and a soft gentle breeze was floating over my naked body, leaving me feeling fresh and alive. I ran my hands over my soft skin, really enjoying my curves for the first time, becoming lost in my mind by my own touch. I felt like a woman, I wanted to embrace that pleasure. A lot of women I had known in the past had hated their curves, but I loved mine. I'd worked hard for them after all, and to some, I might not look that curvy, but to me, any curve was worth showing off. Those other women didn't realise just how lucky they were with the bodies they were born with.

Last night had gone by so very fast, yet so very slow all at the same time. I wanted to relive every moment, to make sure I never forgot. I didn't want the enormity of last night to end and real life to start once again. Not yet, not anytime. Last night everything had just flowed right. I'd never known what that meant before, but last night I really got it. I finally knew what people were talking about when they said you just know, and it just works. There had been a lot of that for me lately, finally getting it. Life that was. We'd not stopped talking at the restaurant, me and him, we had laughed our way through the night, all my previous concerns and questioning about myself just disappeared as we drank wine together and ate fine food. I'd forgotten all about my silly worries about my hands and felt I had really relaxed in his company, more than I had ever done with him up to now, or with anyone else for that matter. I hadn't even planned to do it, to ask him back. If I had thought about it, I might have stumbled over my own words, or talked myself out of it, it was still early days in the relationship in a lot of people's eyes, and I didn't want anyone thinking I was cheap or anything. Plus, there was the slight issue that I hadn't been that honest with him, but I pushed that thought back down again for now, as I had done last night. It hadn't changed things for me, didn't change the way I felt right now, but it might do for him if he really knew.

I closed my eyes and replayed the moment he had first entered my body with his solid strong penis back in my mind. It was a feeling I couldn't put words to, it was a feeling I had been waiting a life time for, it was a feeling that was everything sexually I had ever dreamt of, and that seemed crazy at my age. I tried to forget the little trip I had had to make to the bathroom to sort myself out, trying not to ruin the moment. But I knew natural lubrication was never going to happen for me, and I didn't want to explain that in the heat of the moment. Didn't want to explain why it was essential rather than as a bit of fun. I'd kept a tube in my bathroom cabinet, something I had been experimenting with on myself to see how it all worked, and there I was squeezing it deep into myself for real. It had made me feel so alive and normal, even though in some people's eyes it wasn't normal at all. The alcohol had taken away any fear I might have previously had. I'd been conscious not to overdo it, I wanted it to look natural, I just needed enough to make it all work. I'd hoped my body temperature would warm it up too, to make it feel real. I'd pulled my thong back on and went back to the bedroom, waiting for him to remove them for me. I'd never felt more real than how I felt right at that moment.

I remembered I had let out a little moan as he had pushed himself deep into me. He slid into me so easily and it felt so natural. So complete. The memory sent my hands snaking down to my perfectly formed Vagina, sending a tingle though my entire body and mind once again. I hoped he hadn't noticed how false my lubrication was last night. I knew everyone felt slightly different, but still, I just didn't know. He'd not complained so maybe I did feel normal. I really hoped so, but I couldn't worry about that now. I felt I'd put my childish behaviour from the other week behind me, had shown him how I really felt about him, and shown myself that I had made the right life decision. I just wish he'd not had to go so early this morning; I was ready to make love all over again, and again. I still wanted his body next to mine, I wanted my mind to explode once more

STEVEN JAMES, 2ND JULY 9:30AM

I sat at my desk, taking the occasional glance up from my computer screen to look out over the fully occupied open plan office surrounding and encasing me. I sat almost dead in the middle of the office space, amongst rows and rows of identical soulless desks. You would think it would be a nice quiet working space, the lay out encouraging people to focus on their work, but there was a lot of pointless chatter that went on. Never with me though. People seemed to avoid me, but I couldn't work out why. I could hear my colleague on the next desk talking on the phone to his wife. Every day they had a morning conversation about their child and the school run and making sure the child was happy as the wife left him at the school gates. I didn't get it. It didn't compute in my mind why they couldn't have that conversation later, out of work hours. It made me feel uncomfortable, as we was here to work. At the same time, I was desperate to talk to someone, anyone, who would give me half an hour of their time at lunch to sit and talk in the staff break out area. Looking around there was no one in this busy office that would engage in a conversation with me, let alone a conversation that might possibly involve real life stuff, or emotions. It was like I was invisible. I'd gotten use to the oddity of working here over the years, almost switching off to it, but today it was getting me down.

I sipped my coffee as quietly as I could, I didn't like the thought of people getting annoyed by my sounds, almost chastising myself for being so conformist, but to whom I was conforming to I didn't really know, as no one else seemed to worry about that type of stuff. Realising that this office was all I had in my life, I could have cried. Or shouted. Neither option appropriate right now. The people around me should notice I needed them. I sat in the staff break out area every lunch in the hope that someone would come and join me, hold a conversation with me. To be honest, I doubt any of them would recognise me if they bumped into me in the shops, and if they did, they wouldn't know what to say to me, and to be honest thinking about it now I don't know that I would know what to say to them either.

My friends, the one from my 20's, when everything had been fun and easy, had all disappeared off and settled in difference directions around the country. Engrossed in their marriages, and raising their kids, time was moving fast for them I imagine. Milton Keynes no longer held what they thought they needed to be that perfect family, or it didn't offer them that perfect job. Though I disagreed with that, I thought it had everything I needed, and couldn't think of an easier place to live, but I guess some people just wanted to escape from the place they were raised, to prove they could make it out in the big wide world on their own. Maybe they had it right after all, given my current mood and feelings on life. Could it have been different if I had moved away too. Might I be working somewhere where the people cared? Or was it just me, and it would be the same wherever I was?

The biggest issue I had about my school friends moving away was that it made it difficult to keep in touch with them. The geographical distances between us created such a vast gap that people were too busy to be close, even with the onset of social media the gap seemed to be widening lately. I was a bit old fashioned by my own admission and liked to write letters, on paper. I didn't like pouring my heart out on the internet, for potentially the whole world to see, for people who may not know me to be able to make a judgement on me. I didn't even bother much with writing letters now though, or not with ones that I actually bothered to post anyway. I'd given up getting upset that the people I had shared so many nights out with, holidays, break ups, and weddings couldn't even be bothered to send me a Christmas card anymore. That was one too many wasted emotion, and one had to protect their emotions in life. I had quite a strict order in my head of how things should be, I was slowly realising this could be detrimental to long term happiness though.

Then there was my parents, or rather lack of them. I'd lost them when I was quite young to a car accident. They had been out for the day without me, or I wouldn't be here today by all accounts. I could remember bits about them, but nothing special, or life changing or shaping. I didn't know what their likes and dislikes were, what they liked to eat, what type of films they liked to watch, none of the regular stuff that possibly shapes who you turn out to be. I think at 7 years old, the age I was when they died, you don't take that stuff in about your parents, as the world is all about you at that point in your life. It was quite sad really, as I'd grieved two people I didn't really know. First there was my childhood grieving, almost panic as to what would happen to me, and then there was my adult grieving, which was more of a reflection of what could have been, a childhood lost. It didn't help I was an only child too, so I went through it all alone. But I couldn't complain, I was taken in by a lovely foster family, who later went on to adopt me. You hear of people being passed from pillar to post, in and out of different families, multiple siblings that you might not be related too. There was none of that for me, I stayed as an only adopted child, and as I got older I liked it like that. In a funny sort of way, I just carried on as I was, there was no change, except for the face of who I called mum and dad. Looking back now I'd seemed to take it in my stride, all considering. I guess who I am now is a creation of mum and dad, my adoptive mum and dad, rather than my biological parents. And who I am today, I discovered, was someone who found it hard to admit to anyone just how lonely I had become over the last few years, and how I had turned to the internet to meet that special someone. I'd felt dirty at first, all that scrolling through pages and pages of women's faces, reading their bio's where they tried to sell themselves as 'that one' that you needed. But after a while I'd started to feel a sense of safety with it all, everything was on my terms, and once I'd realised that, it all became fun, like it was meant to be. I could take control over the situation, it could all be within the realms of how I thought things should be, and I could take my time with my replies, make sure that I didn't sound silly, or over keen. I could even add a bit of humour to the conversation, something that didn't come naturally to me when I was face to face with people.

I'd kept my internet fun all to myself for months as I had no one to talk to about it. It became my little escape from the day-to-day formula of the office and work, a formula that usually worked for me, but just sometime even I want to let people in. But now I was sat here at my desk bursting with an excitement I'd not felt in years and I didn't even have one colleague I could share it with. I was that invisible man no one bothered with. Or maybe it was me, maybe I just didn't know how to share it, how to start that conversation with other people. There was a conversation about wife's happening at the desk next to me. Two men were having a laugh and a joke about something silly one of their wife's had done the previous night. I could have joined in, could have said something, but something inside of me stopped me, I didn't know what to say, how to interject, how to join in and be accepted. And part of me had that niggling feeling that they should be having that conversation at lunch, not on works time. With that thought hitting me in the face I realised It was time I change more than just my relationship status.   I needed to change my mind set too.

MICHAEL, 17TH
JULY 11AM

I'd done it. I'd finally made the call I knew I had needed to make for years. I'd finally let my mind admit what I had thought was going on inside it, and I'd made possibly the most important call of my life to date. And now I was sat here, in a bright room with four rows of identical chairs, the type you see in old people's homes, waiting for my name to be called out. They were surprisingly comfortable, the upright chairs, I had noted as I picked at the skin around my left thumb. Nerves were kicking in. I'd thoroughly read all the NHS posters displayed around the room, all stuff I knew, but it kept my mind entertained and my eyes busy as I waited for what felt like ages. The receptionist was busy on the phone trying to diagnose someone's condition, or so it sounded. I'm glad I'd not spoken to her when I'd called to make the appointment. I'd not been in here for years what with being quite a physically fit and healthy person I'd not had the need. It had been that long I'd not actually met my 'family' doctor, as they called it as she'd only joined the practice two years ago. Maybe that fact would make todays conversation easier.

'Michael Cook' I heard a female voice call out my name. I stood, the lady smiled and turned her back to me indicating that I should follow her through to the surgery. Here goes I told myself.

'Take a seat' she pointed to the chair next to her desk as she then took hers which was in front of the desk and computer. She made herself comfortable and then turned to look at me. 'How can I help you today, Michael?' She smiled. It was a lovely smile, caring, like she really did want to help me even though I was just a number in a long line of numbers that she had to get through each day before she could go home.

'This is going to sound mad' I started. 'I don't even know if I am in the right place, but I don't know where else to go. I'm hoping you can help me with that.'

'Try me. I hear all sorts of problems, that's my job, and I'm here to help.' I'm sure she could sense I wasn't in here for the usual aches and pains that she must see more of than she cared to remember.

'For years I've felt that there was something wrong with me, like I was different to everyone else. It's almost like I'm in a different room to everyone else, if you know what I mean? I thought maybe that was just me, that is just how I am, that I am that 'odd' person that seems to be present in most groups.' I started, with a bit of a waffle I know, and insulting to other people, but I didn't know how else to go about it, to describe what I was feeling on the inside. She didn't interrupt, she let me draw breath and carry on.

'You see, I love women, as friends. I've only ever been with women, you know, in the bedroom. But I always just see them as my best friend, so it never works out in the long run. And then I miss them, because I like their company and friendship and how they listen to me, so I start again and meet someone new. I've spiralled like that for years. I know some of my friends call me a player behind my back, but I'm not.' I paused again, the next bit even harder to say out loud to a stranger, albeit a professional stranger. 'I like men too. I have lots of male friends, and I find them more attractive, and sexy, but not in a gay way.' I had to look down at the floor at this point, words that had only ever bounced around inside my head were now out there, in the real world, no going back, in someone else's ear. I didn't want to see any expression on her face, didn't want to see if she approved, or disapproved, or if she just thought I was wasting her time. I was finally speaking out about something that I had trapped and squashed down inside me since I don't know when and I didn't want to feel weird.

'Do you think you might perhaps be gay?' She asked in a gentle way, nothing judgemental with her tone at all, just a simple question. 'As there is nothing wrong with being gay and liking people of the same sex, but it's not a medical condition...'

'NO' I almost shouted at her and cut her off mid-sentence, I hadn't meant to and I felt bad about that. 'Sorry. I didn't mean to shout.' I said, she nodded and let me carry on.

'I know there's nothing wrong with being gay, only I don't think I am gay.' I sighed. 'In fact, I know I am not gay. That's the thing that's been messing me up for years. I've been trying to get over it, see if it was a phase, but I know it's not and it's not going to go away, ever. Life's too short, I want to be me, and I need your help to be able to get there. I think I am trapped.'

'Okay.' She said, interrupting me. I guess my time slot was running out. 'I think the best way forward is to initially refer you for some counselling, which I think might help you make sense of the things that are stuck inside you.' She offered. 'There are trained people who can talk you though your feelings in a more relaxed setting than this surgery can offer. They are specialist too.'

'I don't want it to go away.' I said, maybe not understanding what she was offering, suddenly panicked that she may just want to push this difficult problem under the carpet, fix it quick for her statistics.

I risked glancing up, afraid of what I might see written on her face, but her expression was soft, with a look of genuine concern for my wellbeing. She didn't just want rid of me. I looked around the very medical room I was sat and saw where she was coming from with her suggestion, but I knew I needed to keep talking right now, for a bit anyway. It had been a big effort just to walk through the door, and I didn't want to go home now, not talk about it some more and to have weeks of internal torment whilst waiting for an appointment with a counsellor. I knew though that if I was going to really do something about this, there would be a lot more medical intervention involved at some point, but I needed to talk first, I knew that much. I cast my eyes down to the floor again, took a deep breath, closed my eyes and finally said it out loud to her, the doctor, and to me, my real me.

'I don't think just talking will fully fix it Doctor, no offence. You see, I know I'm not gay. I know I fancy men, and I want nothing more than to be with a man, and I never have been. But the problem is, I don't think I am a man, I think I am a woman trapped in this man's body. Actually, I know I am a woman trapped in this man's body.' I didn't realise I was crying until she handed me a tissue and gently rested her other hand on my shoulder. So many years I'd not wanted to believe it was true, that I was wrong, trying to get over it by myself, but finally saying out loud to another person I felt such relief that I knew it really was true. It was out there in the open, at last. I risked looking up. The Doctor was waiting for me, with a kind eye, and not an ounce of disapproval to be seen.

MICHAEL, 19TH JULY 8AM

It had been two days since my appointment with the doctor, and for the first time in my life I felt real, felt me, and actually felt happy within myself. There was no heavy weight of life being carried on my shoulders. I felt a little bit normal, that was the word I was looking for, and it was something I had been looking for all my life, to just be normal. The Doctor has been wonderful, very caring, and offered me lots of good advice. She made me feel okay about what I had been feeling, and made me realise I wasn't some kind of freak. Her suggestion of counselling was spot on too, I needed to talk, to someone, it was something that was very much needed. I was looking forward to getting started with it to be honest, and not wanting to waste any more of my life living as the wrong person. Thankfully the sessions were starting today. It was only so quick as I'd opted to pay for it, the poor old NHS didn't work that quickly, and I just didn't want to wait any longer now that I had said it out loud. I'd already wasted too many years not being me, and I just couldn't wait to get on with being who I should be. I understood though that before anything else there would need to be some talking. Talking to really get me to understand what was going on inside this head of mine.

I'd called in sick to work too, something I never usually did but I just couldn't face it right now, my masculine role, and the male banter that surrounded me on a day-to-day basis. I just couldn't do it, not today anyway. I didn't know what would happen there as I was good at my job, and I liked it to an extent, but I didn't know if it felt right to be there anymore. And I didn't know how the lads would cope. It was all too much for me to deal with now and it was all too much too soon to think about, and not being there was the easiest thing to do in my mind. They would cope, I'm sure. They would have to.

The worst thing I had done in the last few days though was to hide away from my mother. I'd avoided all her calls and sent her a cowardly text instead. I still needed a bit of time to myself, and some professional support before I tackled speaking to her about it, if I ever did, but I just couldn't cope with her banging on about girlfriends and stuff to me right now. It was a topic of conversation that cropped up during most of our calls, there was no getting her off the subject easily either. But more than anything I needed some space to myself. I couldn't even think about her, my dad or my brothers. I felt a bit sad for her too, she was so proud of me, the me she saw, her son, who had made lots of money and had lots of nice things around him. I'm not sure what my dad thought really, he didn't give much away, or give me much of his time, but I know they both would have liked a wife by my side, and a few grandkids to visit them. Apart from the nagging by phone I think Mum was just happy boasting about me to her friends, her success story, the one they all asked about. This news was going to kill her.

I decided to take the bus to the address I had been given for the counselling session today. The surgery was based in one of the outer towns to Milton Keynes called Stony Stratford. It was a beautiful old town, lots of history and almost a million miles away from the sleek new town I lived in, yet it was only five miles door to door. I could have driven it, I just didn't want to risk my car being seen out on the roads when I should have been in my sick bed resting. I also didn't want my mother seeing my car out as she would only wonder why I wasn't at work and hadn't visited her. My mother never took the bus anywhere, far too dirty for her, so there was no risk of bumping in to her on route, and I don't think she ventured out of town, the glitzy City Centre shops offering her all she thought she needed in life. In fact, I don't think I knew anyone who would be out this way, on a bus, so I felt pretty safe.

I stepped off the bus, glad to get out into the fresh air for a moment. The building I was heading for was a short five-minute walk from the bus stop, and I still had half an hour until my appointment time to spare. I stopped off in a little newsagent and brought myself a bottle of water, and a pack of tissues. I could feel the tears brewing already and I'd not even sat in a counselling chair yet. I think some of it was apprehension, some of it was relief, and if I'm honest some of it was shear fright about what the future might hold for me right now. I was keen to know how it all might happen too. I had so many questions bouncing around my head and I wanted it all to happen as soon as it could, I don't think I was going to like waiting! I'd never had any counselling of any description before in my life and I just didn't know what to expect from this session yet alone the future.

I walked along the street checking the door numbers as I passed each front door until I found the number I was looking for. I took a deep breath and walked up the steps to the heavy black door. It was the right address but the signage outside was very discrete. You'd miss it if you didn't know what was here and wasn't looking for it. I know I'd walked down this street before and just thought this was an ordinary house on the main road nestled in with all the other ordinary houses with similar heavy black doors. I pushed the door open, half expecting it to be locked, and this to be the wrong door or house, but it gave way and opened onto a large airy reception. The reception area was very welcoming with flowers on the desk, nice lighting and chairs all placed in a welcoming way that you could sit on your own, but not be hidden. No looking straight at other patients here, wondering what was going on with them, no NHS posters about the flu jab and the importance of washing your hands all the time. If fact, I could have been sat in a nice hotel lobby it was that relaxing, and I began to wonder if I was. I guess that's what we were all paying for, that comfort, that niceness, that bit of discretion. I didn't have to wait long either in my nice relaxed chair, my name was called, and I stood up and made my way towards the man that had called me, he waited for me to reach him, shook my hand, said hello and introduced himself before showing me the way to the room where we could talk. I guess that's what you call it, a room rather than a surgery. I didn't know, this was all a bit new but it didn't really matter either. An odd thought occurred to me as I followed him along the long corridor... I might not be Michael for much longer.

MIA, 23RD JULY 8PM

I was feeling excited about tonight, and I just couldn't keep still. Me and my man were off out on a date again. It had been so long since I last saw him it sort of feels like I'm getting ready for that first date all over again, complete with the butterflies. My busy diary and his busy diary had totally clashed, and this was our first meet up since 'that' day. I had started to think I had totally blown it with him, maybe we had taken that step in our relationship too soon, it was something that had played on my mind ever since we had slept together. I'd had used every technique taught to me to prevent my mind spiralling towards paranoid thoughts that I would struggle to come back from. The thought that it was me, that I had done something wrong, that it was all my fault, which in a way I know I had done something very wrong. I know that would seem a bit over the top to most people, so I'd not shared that thought with anyone else, I'd just kept it locked inside of me and tried to appear happy and normal to the outside world. Actually, the only people I had really seen since that night were the girls at work, and whist I got on with them really well, and they were good fun to work with, it was clear I wasn't fully part of their tight nit group just yet. Things were getting better though, slowly, but I wasn't ready to share all my thoughts, fears and feelings with them, especially within the confines of the office. I hadn't yet reached social invite status to even consider telling them anything important anyway. They didn't even know I had been dating someone. I think they sort of saw me as the quiet girl in the corner they could off load their problems on too, yet I don't think they even gave it a second thought that I even had a life, feelings and worries of my own outside of work. It might be partly my fault as I didn't volunteer much information to them freely, and they never asked me any return questions about myself, they were all so self-absorbed in their own lives. It worked for me though, and I was happy with it that way most of the time.

The doorbell dinged loudly bringing me back into the present moment with a thump. He was picking me up from home tonight in the taxi, which was very gentlemanly of him, and made me feel looked after and protected, it was a nice feeling to have. I risked glancing in the mirror as I passed by it to make sure I looked okay, but it was too late to do anything about it if I didn't as he was now sat waiting for me. Annoyed at myself for not taking this glance sooner, but relieved to see my makeup was still in place and looked good I headed to the door, and his waiting car. I'd reduced my makeup levels a little bit too, to try and present a softer image, something I'd read suggested 'less is best. 'I hope he liked it as I felt a bit exposed.

'Hello Stranger' he greeted me with a big smile and open arms. We embraced and pecked each other on the cheek, as people do.

'Hello' I replied back. 'You look nice' as he did. I'd forgotten how much I fancied him.

'As do you. You look different, have you changed your hair?'

Typical man, I thought, but that was good. He didn't spot the finer details of my makeup, the colour of my nails, the actual details of my hair, he just noticed something overall that he liked with my image, I hoped. But had noticed something was different, and in my experience if a man noticed that 'something' that was a good start and was 'someone' to hold onto. It worked for me, but I didn't want to bore him with the finer details like some girls did and would with their men if they made a similar compliment to them. That 'you look different' was not an invite to talk about hair and make up for half an hour, it was just an actual compliment, just take it and leave it there. That was a lesson I had tried to give to the girls at work, but they didn't think I knew what I was talking about, I know they chose to nod politely and ignore me on that one. Little did they know.

'Sort of changed something.' I smiled. 'Let's go and get that drink though, we have so much to catch up on.' I couldn't wait to get out from the four walls of my house, and the confines of my street and enjoy being in the big wide world again. It had felt too long being stuck in that house of mine.

We went to a town called Stony Stratford. There were lots of different places to drink, but in a slightly more chilled setting to the main town of Milton Keynes. I'd suggested it, I'd been wanting to come here for a night out for a while, and tonight seemed like the perfect night to explore the town's pubs. I'd only ever ventured here by day before, and when the taxi dropped us off I was quite surprised by how busy the place was of an evening. Not in an unpleasant way at all, there was a good vibe to the high street as people meandered from pub to pub enjoying the warm summer evening. We walked along hand in hand, I felt so proud, people looking at us, not knowing our stories, just seeing two people who looked in love, who looked like they were a couple and who looked happy.

'Let's try in here.' He gestured to the open door of The Cock Hotel. The bar area looked full enough to not be too quiet, but I could see an empty table in the corner. We made our way over to it and took our seats to reserve them, then he went and brought a bottle of wine for us to share, he didn't even need to ask me which one I wanted, he knew my wine taste very well already. There was something about him looking after me like that that I liked, he took control and made it easy for me. It was a feeling I wanted to experience more of.

He sat back down and poured us both a glass. 'Cheers.' We chimed each other's glasses and the conversation from that point flowed so easily, it was like I had only just seen him yesterday. We shared work stories from the last few weeks, both interested in what each other had to say or moan about. It sounded like he wasn't that happy at work, and we talked about that for quite a bit of the night. It took me off course from what I had wanted to talk to him about, but if I was honest with myself, I was looking for any old excuse not to go down that line with him, just yet anyway. And as always with him, the evening seemed to come to an end far too soon. At the start of the night we had planned on a little bar crawl, but when the bar staff at The Cock rang the bell for last orders it became apparent we were a bit too late for the crawling to begin.

'Shall we grab a late-night curry?' he asked. 'Soak up the three bottles of wine we've managed to down?' He winked.

I wouldn't normally go for a curry, especially so late at night, not any more anyway. I was so conscious of my weight, and keeping my shape as slim as I could, that late night food has been taken off my 'approved' list. We had drunk a lot though, and I'd not eaten much today so this one time it was probably a good idea, and it had the added benefit of prolonging the night with him too. 'OK, I'm up for that.' I replied, already planning what I could eat with the least number of calories in at this late hour. What I should really be planning was talking to him about the thing I really needed to talk to him about, but my inner self decided that a public curry house wasn't the place to confront it anyway, far too 'public', and that old self of mine came through and buried that thought and my head deep into the sand once more. There was always another day I told myself.

The curry turned out really nice, my body was telling me it was actually very much needed. I'd gone for a Tikka, mainly because it had no sauce. I could eat it tidily, always an issue or rather a concern for me, and it was probably the better option for my weight as it was just meat. I didn't have a rice, too messy, and I just didn't fancy too much food really. I couldn't say what he had, my head was a little spiny and I was so focussed on my meal, and how I looked eating it that all I saw on his plate was a large amount of food. I knew that could only mean one thing, he might struggle to stay awake once we got to bed. That much food, and that much drink is a known winning combination for a good sleep. I was a little disappointed but tried not to show it and I just hoped he wasn't that typical a man after all. The waiting staff cleared away our plates and he paid the bill, all of a sudden, the end of the night seemed to gather a momentum that I couldn't stop. Before I knew it, he was calling a cab for us and that was that night out done.

'I can't stay tonight.' He said quietly as we stood side by side on the pavement outside the curry house waiting for the cab. He was still holding my hand tenderly, as if he was trying to let his statement filter into my subconscious mind so that I didn't assume or ask him to stay. I felt a complete fool, as that is exactly what I had done, assumed he would be coming back home with me after our night out, that we would wake in the morning in each other's arms like all the other couples I had seen out during the evening would be. I fought to keep the hurt from bubbling up and presenting itself as tears, that wouldn't do me or the situation any good. Afterall, I was a grown woman and not a child that had just been told they weren't going to the play park that day.

'Okay no worries' I responded, trying not to sound too breezy about it, yet trying not to sound too hurt. Thankfully he couldn't see my face, I knew if he could he would see how I really felt as it was written all over it. I really thought he would be coming back to mine, assumed he would want to repeat what had happened the other week between us, I know I wanted too, desperately. It's all I had been thinking about for weeks now. I'd even prepped myself in the toilets at the curry house, so that I didn't need to make excuses to do it at home, I felt like a fool with wet nickers. To get rid of my looming tears I faked a sneeze, least I could easily explain the redness in my eyes now.

'Bless you.' He fumbled in his pocket, dragging out a hanky

which he handed to me. 'It's just I've got to work tomorrow; this project is really taking over my life at the moment. It will go live soon, then I get my life back.' He was facing me now. I could see he was being genuine, a slight concern on his face questioning how pissed off I really was, and why my eyes were that red just from one sneeze.

Another assumption on my part, with it being a Friday, I thought he wouldn't be working tomorrow which is why I had suggested it was tonight that we met up. 'we'll have to celebrate go live then.' I said with a smile, trying to cover my hurt and come across as my usual bubbly self. 'I'll cook you a nice dinner.' The words tumbled out of my mouth before I could stop them. Gulp. He might take me up on that, I almost held my breath.

He smiled. 'You're on.' He said. 'Gives me something to look forward too.' He then gave me a kiss.

I wasn't sure if he would be so happy about it once the dinner had been served though, and not because of the food I would place on his plate. I knew that would be very tasty, even if I did say so myself. I realised once the words were out of my mouth and out in the open the real sticking point of the night would be that 'dinner night' would be the night I would need to talk to him, to be honest with him, to tell him the truth. I needed to, if this relationship was going to turn into something real and meaningful, something long term. I needed to tell him before we both got hurt. No more pretending and hiding just because it suited me, those days needed to be behind me now.

We got into the cab and we held hands across the back seat like new lovers would. The conversations returned to that easy chatter we had been enjoying all night. My stomach started to settle as we weaved our way across the town towards my house. He was being gentlemanly dropping me off first, and I again enjoyed the feeling of being looked after and protected, even though it would have been easier and cheaper to go to his house first, and I would have actually been alright in a cab on my own. Our goodbyes were that of just friends, another quick peck on the cheek so as not to offend or embarrass the taxi driver. With a 'see you soon then' from him as I got out the cab, and no actual date set. I was left with a sad-ish flat feeling I couldn't put my finger on. This time I let the tears quietly flow as I opened the front door to my quiet empty house. I felt a fool as I made my way to the bathroom to sort myself out, my knickers now a mess with a dampness that had no use. I tidied myself up, put clean underwear on and my old favourite pyjamas. Even though the night was warm I felt a chill and needed the comfort of their soft lining to help me get to sleep. I climbed into bed and waited for sleep to take me to a safe place, whilst the awake me thought about my life, the changes that I had made to it, and if it had all really been worth losing my family and friends over. I think if I had a network of people around me I wouldn't feel so desperate about me new love. I didn't want him to see that I was desperate for him, I didn't want him to change his mind. I don't think I could face losing another person from my life because of decisions I had made about me. My eyes started to feel heavy, I was slowly dropping off, drifting out of the conscious day, grateful for that at least.

MICHAEL, 20TH JULY 11AM

The counselling had been the best experience of my life to date, and that sounded crazy even to me, especially considering the places I had travelled to over the years, the envy of many of my school friends with the things I had had the opportunity to do and see. The counsellor had really let me open up and talk freely, he hadn't doubted me or my feelings for one second. He hadn't suggested it was a phase I might be going through, like I thought he might have done, and he hadn't suggested that I might be gay, which was a relief as I didn't want to defend that one again. He didn't approve, or disapprove of anything I said, he just let me to talk, and he just listened for the most part. When he did finally speak his suggestions on the way forward for me made absolute sense. It was the first time a 'plan' had ever felt like a plan that I wanted to be part of, as it was a plan that was all about the real me. We'd made an appointment for a weeks' time and he sent me away with some homework, as I'd come to him quite raw it turns out. I didn't care what his fee was, I was spending money on something that meant a lot to me, and he was that good he was worth every penny.

The biggest thing that I had taken away from my session with the counsellor was that I needed to start living as the new me, and this was my first homework task that had been set. A big leap, but was it really? I took his very well made point.

Apparently, a lot of people go to him having already taken that important first step, had dabbled and tried stuff out behind a closed door, but I'd not done any of that, which was unusual it seems. Everything had been so deeply buried within me I'd not considered experimenting. I needed to get rid of the old me, start to say goodbye to him, and embrace the new me, the real me that had been hidden for so long. I know it's going to be hard to start with, but I know I need to do it, and more than anything I really want to do it. With my homework fresh in my mind, and my new life waiting to start, I decided that the charity shops in this little town was going to be the perfect place to begin my journey and to start that 'dabbling.' Whilst they maybe didn't stock my dream idea of lady's fashion, partly due to their suppliers, they did offer something else that was far more important to me right now than fashion itself. The shops were generally small, and safely away from the main shops where most people were drawn to, including my mother. On top of that they were often staffed by older ladies who just loved to help anyone and everyone and loved a good natter at the same time. I didn't know anything about dress sizes for my manly bulk and wouldn't have known where to start in a main stream shop, but a little white lie about a 'fancy-dress' party had had the woman in the shop flocking round me to find that suitable dress, handbag and surprisingly shoes for that 'party' I was going to at the weekend. I felt a bit mean lying to the ladies in the shop as they all seemed so genuine in their efforts to help me, but it needed to be one step at a time with facing the world at the moment and if a white lie got me there I'm sure I could be forgiven for it. Plus, I didn't want my life becoming the hot gossip of this small town, I wanted them to forget me the second I walked out if their shop. And when I did finally walk out of the shop I was rather pleased with myself to be fair. I had a full head to toe outfit to experiment with and all of it for the small sum of £30.00. I couldn't wait to get home to try them all on again, in private, so I could really take it all in, and for the first time to be able to really have a good look at myself.

***

It was now 24 hours on from my appointment in Stony Stratford, and I had not left the house at all. As soon as I'd gotten indoors yesterday I had put my 'fancy dress' outfit on and had then spent the rest of the day in it. I love my new clothes, I love the feeling they give me when I'm walking about, and to see myself in the mirror makes my heart leap. I'm enjoying taking it all in, I have no need to get changed and go out. I'd even slept in these clothes last night, but that was okay, this outfit would never venture out into the streets for public viewing. And not because I had changed my mind, this was just not the outfit to do it in. I keep looking at myself in the mirror as I walked about the house. I love the way the skirt part of the dress looks against my newly shaved legs. And the shoes felt wonderful. I liked the tightness of them as they hugged my feet within their narrow leather confines. I set my phone against a pile of magazine and hit record, so I could film myself walking about in them. I wanted to be able to see how I looked, from another person's view. Apparently, according to the lady in the charity shop, these were classed as a 'kitten heel' and not as difficult to walk in as a stiletto might be. It still wasn't a pretty sight to be fair, and it was not how I was visualising myself at all. I had thought I was being all elegant, but it was evident that 'elegance' would take some time and practice. I was glad I had taken the lady's advice on the shoe height to be honest, I'd have to build up to something a little higher and sexier in time, maybe. Or maybe kitten heels would be my preferred option, who knows.

There was one thing I wasn't liking the look of in the mirror though, and that was my short manly hair. I know it would take time to grow, but I was impatient, and I wanted something more instant to complete my new look and make me not look like the old me. As with a lot of things of late, Google became my best friend for the afternoon. I sat glued to the computer screen deep in research looking for my new hair which would be in the form of a wig. It was the only option I had open to me, for that instant change at least. But I'd never realised what a large industry the wig world was. There were so many options it was hard to know what to go for, especially when I couldn't physically try them on to see what they looked like or how they felt even. In the end I went for a more expensive one, made with real hair that would sit below my shoulders, hopefully. It would have probably been better to go to a store and try on a few, but that would take too much explaining at this early stage, and I just wasn't ready for that. I liked the anonymity the internet gave me, it's safety net worth the risk of buying the wrong thing. I didn't think the 'fancy dress party' story would work when you're spending £400.00 on a wig supposedly for one night out, and I thought the local shops might only have cheap party ones in stock anyway for 'fancy dress'. I wanted something that looked like I had grown it myself, so I was happy to spend the extra money. My new hair, close in colour to my own, would be with me in two to three working days, and that was fine. I could wait that long for it. Now to the next thing on my homework list, I needed to order some make up so that I could try and hide the old me. That's not what they had said at my appointment, rather that it might help me feel more like a woman. But I saw it as hiding the old me, from me. And with my dark complexion I think I might have to order serious heavy-duty stuff to be fair. I haven't got a clue when it comes makeup though, it's all a bit of a mine field. I'd not had sisters that I could have learnt from, like kids do when they are young, boys and girls alike end up covered in the stuff for fun. And my mother had always been very minimal when it came to makeup so I could never pick tips up from her. Minimal wasn't going to cut it for me.

Google wasn't so friendly or helpful on this bit of research sadly. I think it was probably more a user error on my part than anything else though. I'd never realised just how much stuff you could buy to put on your face, and I just didn't know where to begin with it. There were primers, foundations, powers, all in one's, blushers, eye liners and shadows and then there was the lipstick options…. The list went on. Literally hundreds of colours to suit every complexion, colour and skin type out there, only I didn't know what my complexion was, or what my skin type was. How do woman know this stuff? Do they go to secret classes to learn about it? I was scrolling down the list of foundations… a good starting point I thought. Being white I thought there would be the white person option for skin shade… oh no, there are different shades of white…. I always thought white was just white, but apparently not. I just didn't know what I needed but on the other hand there was a part of me having so much fun looking, now I had that green light to be able too. Four hours later I was still browsing, and with nothing in my on-line basket I could be a few more hours with this yet. I didn't want to look like a clown or anything so I decided that I perhaps the best option would speak to the counsellor about it during the next visit. Professional help was needed on this one I think.

My phone beeped signalling a text had just come through. It brought me back to the here and now. I picked it up wondering who it could be, all thoughts of reality had left me whilst I had been lost in my makeup world, it took me a few moments to focus on reality. I looked at my screen, and my body went cold. It was her, my latest girlfriend, wanting to know if I wanted to meet up with her later. I didn't know how I would tackle this situation, but I know I needed too. I started to type it all out, what had been going on with me, and that I couldn't see her like 'that' anymore, then had second thoughts and rapidly deleted it all from the screen. I liked her a lot, as a person, and I saw her as a good friend. I owed her face to face if nothing else. I didn't want her to think she had done something wrong, I wanted her to be able to walk away with her head held high, and I didn't want my actions to affect her confidence or anything for her life as she moved on from me. So, I did the only thing I could do and I arranged to meet up with her in a few days' time for a drink. Once we'd made the arrangements the biggest decision I had was did I turn up as me, Michael, or did I turn up as the new me, still with no name? I didn't know what the right thing was to do, and I had no one to ask about it either. I still had my phone in my hand and without really thinking about it a randomly Googled the question, not really expecting an answer. A link came up that looked interesting, it was a forum for transitioning! Life really did seem to be all about the internet at the moment. I quickly created myself an account and entered the site to see what it was about, hoping to find someone who I could talk too. And I did. It was faceless, but it was just what I needed.

After a bit of chat with someone I only knew as 'Liz', who made some very valid points, I decided that I should meet up with my girlfriend as the old me, Michael, the one she knew and had been falling for. On reflection 'Michael' probably had a few face to face trips he needed to make before I could put him to bed for the last time, so to speak. Liz had pointed out that I needed to be fair and respectful to my family and friends and think about their feelings too, as they didn't know this was going on in my head, and I think Liz was right there. Especially when I would need my family for all the support they could offer over the coming months. Turning up as a woman to tell them probably wasn't the best idea. This 'thing', whatever it was, the thing that had gone wrong inside with my making, it had been with me a while, if not my entire life, but to others this was going to be a shock and something totally out of the blue. My parents were on that list to visit as Michael, I was their son after all, and turning up as the new me without warning seemed a tad unfair and cruel on them, and rather selfish of me. Liz ha pointed out too that I was their son, their first-born son at that, and that really, I should talk to them first before I start telling other people, and especially before the date with my girlfriend. Liz had pointed out that news travels fast, in any town, and how would I feel if it had got back to my parents somehow before I had had the chance to see them and tell them directly. That had the potential to break even the strongest of relationships, even more so given the subject matter. I text my mum right then to see when she would be free. She came back to me straight away. I too replied straight back to her, before I could change my mind and have seconds thoughts. We arranged to see each other the following morning.

I didn't know too much about Liz, I didn't know where she lived, if she was fully trans, what she looked like, or anything, but I really liked her, she had let me type freely, and had made some very good points and suggestions which stopped me making more of a mess of things than what they might be. She was amazing, she had done it in a way that I felt like I was chatting to someone I had known for ages. I had created a whole image in my head of what she was like in real life. Do people make friends they then go on to meet in real life on these forums, I didn't know, I'd never been on one before, but I did hope that I would get to talk to her again soon, and I hoped I could be of help to her if she needed me, I didn't want it to be all one sided.

MICHAEL, 21ST JULY 10AM

I was still off sick from work. There was too much going on inside my head, and I just needed some space from everyone and everything. I was owed a lot of time anyway so the bosses didn't mind too much, for now anyway. I'd just have to figure the rest out as I went along, one hurdle at a time and all that. And today's hurdle was my mother. At least I'd not had too long to panic and over think it and talk myself out of going to see her at all. I felt so nervous about seeing her, but that was silly. She'd always said her love for me was unconditional, that nothing I could do would ever change that… well, I was about to test that statement and see how far unconditional really went.

I pulled my car onto her drive, my tyres crunching against the newly laid gravel, a sound I wasn't at all that keen on in all honesty, but one that my mother loved. She thought it signalled rich to those around her, and she did like the neighbours to think they were doing OK for themselves. I'd never argued that point with her that it could work the other way, being that stuck up. She was happy in the bubble she seemed to live in and she was still my mum, I didn't want to upset her. Not about that anyway. My mother was a very proud lady, too proud for her own good. Everything had to be 'just right', often at the sacrifice of all else. She couldn't have her friends or neighbours thinking badly of her, or risk them saying anything negative about her to each other behind her back. So, my father had arranged for the gravel to be put down, along with a new posh gate, which she had kindly left open for my arrival, and anything else she wanted. He never said no to her, I don't think he knew how. I noted that the lawn was as immaculate as ever, complete with its own set of stripes, and all the flowers were all standing to attention, they daren't droop or they were for the chop. That was a funny thought, the chop, I thought to myself, given what might be happening to me in the near future. Least I knew I still had my sense of humour!

'Darling.' My mother greeted me with open arms as I got out of my car. 'What a pleasant surprise, a mid-week visit from my biggest boy. No work today darling?'

I didn't like to point out it wasn't really a surprise as we'd text yesterday to confirm our meet up, but stopped myself, realising I was just getting tetchy knowing the real reason behind my visit, and she was always the same so why pick her up on it now.

'No dad?' I asked, avoiding answering her questions just yet.

'No, he's off at one of his clubs today.'

'Oh, I thought he might have stayed in as I was coming over.' But I don't know why I thought that, he never had before, why would he think this was a special or important visit and stay home to see me. Mum would just have to tell him, like she had done with everything else that had happened in mine and my brothers lives over the years. He wasn't what you would call an involved dad. Maybe it was a generation thing, maybe it was just the way he was. It hadn't made for a deep relationship between us though.

'Don't be like that, you know he doesn't like to miss anything.' She said as she took my arm and guided me in to the house. Mother didn't like any kind of upset being discussed outside the house, where there was a risk that one of the neighbours might hear which could then ruin their elution of her perfect life.

'Beside.' She continued once she had closed the front door behind us. 'It means I get you all to myself.' She gave me a big hug, before pointing at my feet for me to remove my shoes. We couldn't have outside shoes across the carpet, a habit I had picked up from my mother, but one that I had let slip over the last few days in my own house as more important issues had taken over my life. My mother then guided me to her kitchen, her favourite place for morning entertaining. The room was part kitchen and part conservatory and had a very light and airy feel to it. They had designed it themselves when they had had the extension done, and it was my mother's favourite room. Too be fair it was probably my favourite room in their house too, and the one where I spent most time when I visited them. Lots of happy family memories had been made in this room, and I was about to make another lasting memory for her that might change her feelings about this room in the future, and about me forever.

'Shall I pop the kettle on?' she asked but was doing it already.

'Go one then. Guess it's too early for a glass of wine?' I joked.

'Michael... yes, it is!' She sort of joked back, but there was seriousness behind her response which let me know she wasn't impressed with day time drinking, and she hoped it wasn't something that I took part in.

She placed the two cups of coffee on coasters on the glass table and made herself comfortable on the leather stool besides me. She swivelled it round so she was facing me; I could sense she wanted to be near me.

'So, did I tell you about Lynne down at number 9.....' she started with her usual updates on the street, none of which I ever really cared about, and even less so today. But I let her waffle on, get it out of her system, before we got down to talking about me. She would never change, today wasn't the day to try and encourage her, it was going to be hard enough for her in a moment, I thought I'd let her enjoy a bit of a light gossip, before she became the gossip.

'Are you listening to me Michael... did you hear what I said about Lynne? You look like you're a million miles away!' She struggled to hide the annoyance in her voice.

That was my chance, but I just said 'Sorry mum, what was you saying? How is Lynne?' Some habits are hard to break I guess, especially with the ones who we use to be attached to by an apron string.

We were now onto our second cup of coffee, and I still hadn't broached the subject that I had come to talk to her about. My nerves were kicking in and I felt quieter than normal around her but my mum was still under the impression I was on annual leave from work and that I was some kind of doting son who wanted to use his leave up drinking coffee in his mother's kitchen just for fun, she didn't seem to notice my quietness at all. I wouldn't usually mind, it was often the same, I would sort of go unnoticed once I was sat down with a coffee, which I didn't mind as that's the way it was, but today there was an actual reason for me being here. I needed to be strong and just get on and tell her. I still needed my mum, no matter what I might say, and I desperately wanted to know that she was going to be there for me. There was going to be a tough enough journey ahead as it was.

'Mum. I need to talk to you about something.' I spat it out, cutting her off mid flow about Janet, another neighbour. I wasn't able to wait any longer.

'Oh no, don't tell me you've got this new girlfriend of yours pregnant, and you're not even married to her!! What will people say?! And your father, he won't be impressed I can tell you that now.'

I didn't want to point out that she had put general people above my father, there was nothing new there, but for some reason it really irritated me right now. What if I had got a girlfriend pregnant, what would it matter to her, or the neighbours, as long as we both loved and cared for the child. And I had already proved that wasn't an issue. Okay, it might make the real me coming out a lot harder if I did have another child on the way, but that would be the only problem I could see, and that would be my problem to deal with, not my mothers, and not anyone else's.

'No mother. I've not got anyone pregnant, but how do you feel about having a daughter instead?' I spat it out as I was a bit annoyed with her, irritation getting the better of me, I hadn't meant it to sound quite like that.

'You're getting married?! That's very soon Michael, you've not known her long, and we've not even met her, but it's about time you settled down, so I am okay with it.' She announced, totally misunderstanding what I had meant, and totally belittling me, again. Like I needed her approval if I did decide to get married.

'No mother, I'm not getting married! That would be a daughter IN LAW.' I was struggling to hide the irritation in my voice, exaggerating the final part of my sentence a little bit too much. 'I'm trying to tell you that I am a woman mum, trapped inside a man's body. And I've been stuck in this man's body all of my life.' I left if to hang there, my mother looking at me in total confusion not really grasping or understanding what I, her SON, had just told her. This was not something that happened in her world, or the world of her precious friends, this was something she might watch on television, but even then, probably not, I don't think it's a subject matter she would think to learn about as it wasn't something she would want in her life. We sat there just staring at each other, neither one daring to speak for fear of what might come out next. And then her head dropped, and then she cried. I tried to hold her hand, to comfort her and let her know it was okay, I was still me, but she pulled her hand from mine, leaving my manly hand on the glass table all alone. Which is exactly how I felt in the world right now. All alone.

Today had gone worse than I had expected. I wish I could turn the clock back and try again, another more gentle way.

STEVEN JAMES, 28TH JULY 11AM

W ork had totally consumed every ounce of my being and soul for what felt like far too long, especially as all my hard work didn't seem to get me any further up the internal work ladder, the top being where I had set my sights on. I found the work rewarding and I use to think that was enough in life, that work was my life, and that's why I tried so hard. But those feelings had changed, gradually, over the last few years, and I don't' feel so passionate about it all so much now. I had tiny glimpses of time when I actually felt like I'd made a difference to someone's life through the course of my work, and the odd 'thank you' that I received from clients left me with a temporary mild high feeling. But none of that lasted, those moments were always followed by big voids of silence, loneliness and a total feeling questioning why did I bother with any of it as I wasn't progressing as quickly up that ladder as I would have liked. That had all changed recently though. Work was still the same, sadly no physical change there, and no promotion yet either, but how I dealt with it all in my mind is what had changed for me. The silence towards me from my colleagues was the first thing I tackled, as it had been a bug bare of mine since day one at this job. I didn't want people's avoidance of me bringing down my new-found happiness feeling that I had outside of this building. A nice discreet pair of headphones had been the answer to that little problem, filling my head with sounds of what I wanted to hear, filling m y head with sound full stop. I only wore one of the earpieces though, so I could still hear if on that rare occasion someone needed to come and talk to me about something. But the gentle music in my ears had helped me relax and not get wound up by the people around me. I had my choice of sound in my head, it helped me focus, more than anything else. The second thing I tackled was the actual people. Okay, I didn't actually 'tackle the people' I worked with per say, but I tackled my mind set on how I dealt with the people around me in general. Once I realised that half of them probably felt the same way that I did, and we were all just trying to get through the day in the best way we could, it helped me put it all into perspective a little. I started to let go of the annoyances I had been harbouring about them all and began focussing on the important stuff... my real life, the one outside of this office. That's what really mattered at the end of a working day when the office door closed behind me, and I stepped forth into the world. It had taken me a long time and a lot of thinking to come to this realisation, but it had been worth the effort of going through that thought process, for me anyway.

I was so happy with the way my real life was going right now that I had sort of put-on hold changing my job. I'd gone through the effort of updating my CV but didn't send the e-mail to the recruitment agency asking them to put me on their books. I felt I deserved more from my career for the level of input I offered this place, and it just wasn't forthcoming but, I had this odd theory in life that I didn't want to jinx. I believed that there must always be something that's not quite perfect in life, you can't ever have 100% happiness. There was always that one person at work who annoyed everyone else, the one who everyone couldn't wait to hear the news they had handed their notice in, but then that annoying person goes and leaves, and ends up being replaced by the next annoying person. Or you have that amazing job, but your house is in a less desirable neighbourhood. Or you might have loads of money, but your boss won't let you take any time off to be able to enjoy it. Whatever 'it' is, there is always something that makes life run at 95% happiness, and that was being generous in my mind, and by my own personal experience. My friends, the ones from my youth, all called me a pessimist when we all still hung out, saying I always saw that negative side in everything, but I didn't think that was the case. I believed I had a more realistic view on the bigger picture than them. On our very rare meetups since we all went our separate ways, a couple of them seemed to have their own pessimistic views on things now too... kids, marriage, mortgages all taking their toll on their sunny outlooks. Although they were happy, I could tell they were now at 95% satisfaction like me, though I never pointed this out to them for fear of being shouted down. The meet ups were so rare now I wouldn't want to ruin the moment, even for the sake of making a point to them. I liked and missed them too much for that.

So that was where I was at. My personal life had taken a complete 180-degree turn around, and I was the happiest I had been in years, I figured work was that 5% of negative stuff that I needed to keep in my life so that I could keep other bad stuff at bay, and I just had to get on and deal with it. I didn't want to risk my personal happiness if suddenly I found that new amazing job that I loved. Up to now, although the job was as it was, it had been better than my home life by far which is why I had always thrown myself in to it. Even being ignored by the people around me was still being in the company of people, and there had been weeks when these people I worked with had been the only people I'd had any contact with full stop. Plus, my head was spinning so much these days, I was struggling to concentrate on anything at all, she has turned my world upside down, my internet lady. I feel alive, excited, giddy, it's all going on inside of me and I am finding it a little confusing and exciting, it's a feeling I love. Emotions I had never felt before were taking priority in my mind, and I didn't want to push them away now or ever. I was generally quite an emotionless person; I had had to be over the years since I was a child. I found it all a bit weird having all these feelings in my body and mind, but it was a nice weird even for me. At least with the job I am currently doing I know what is expected of me, I can do it with my eyes shut, learning something new was out of the question right now, I just don't think I could cope with anything more.

Our 'dates' and opportunities to meet up were still a little bit sporadic for my liking, but I was conscious that I didn't want to look too keen and scare her off. It had taken me so long to meet someone that I really liked, and that seemed to like me back in return. She didn't seem to care about my odd ways and outlook on things, I felt like I had finally met someone who got me. I wanted to hold on to her, didn't want to let this opportunity slip through the net, and I didn't want to start over looking for someone new now. I knew I wasn't everyone's cup of tea, even if I didn't admit that out loud. Its' what had put me off opening up to people too soon in the past, but it did feel so different with her. She's so easy to talk to, and she doesn't seem to make any judgement on or about me. It feels like I have always known her, or that I know her better than I actually do. But still, I didn't want to overdose her with me too soon, so I'm sort of holding back, and am sort of busy with work at the same time so it's an easy hold back to do. I don't know if this is the right way to play it, but it's what feels right for me, so who cares as long as she is okay with it. Those days in-between seeing her though, they feel like a lifetime. I count the hours until we next meet, play music that reminds me of her, and basically just think about her during my every waking moment. And that is where I am at right now. Listening to music from my one earphone sat at my work desk as I replay every moment of our last date in my mind in a dreamy state. It was all very unlike me; I almost didn't recognise my behaviour as me. I play back things in my head she'd said to me, and how I had responded, making sure I haven't said anything too silly, hadn't seemed too keen, but been keen enough at the same time. Saying goodbye that night had been hard, I knew it would be days before we could meet up again, and I hadn't wanted to leave her that night but I was trying to be sensible. I wish there was a guide book on how to do this dating thing, I really didn't want to mess it up. I made a mental note to look on Amazon for a book or something, there must be someone who has written a 'How To Guide' on it all for people like me, there seemed to be books on everything else these days.

Apart from my friends from my younger years, I'd never really felt I could be me and let go with anyone else before. My friends, the ones who had grown up with me, from a time when society and social etiquette didn't play the part it does for an adult, were all use to me and my funny ways. They were very good at putting me in my place if I needed it and weren't afraid to either. But I wasn't sure I could accept that honesty from anyone else other than them, so had I struggled with new people all my adult life. To let someone in close enough to get to the stage where they needed to put me in my place was just too much for me to cope with. I'd often wondered if all my old friends had moved away because of me and my difficult ways. I know that's a silly self-indulgent thought, but it's a thought that creeped into my mind from time to time none the less. One of them had told me that too, that I was being too dramatic and self-obsessed in moment of self-pitying and doubt that I'd had shared with him one drunken night. I sometimes needed to be told, it always put me back on the right track. I still missed my friends, and the support they gave me, and it was often in my low moments of missing them I'd slip back into that dark place of 'it's all because of me that they moved away, I drove them away.' Thankfully I was nowhere near that dark place right now, I'm on cloud nine, somewhere where I have never been. I want to do everything I can to stay up here too, as I'm quite enjoying it. I wish I could ring one of my old friends now, and tell them all about what's been happening, be excited about it with someone, show them I can do it, but I'm not that brave, I'm not one for boasting about the good things.

MICHAEL, 29TH
JULY 6PM

It had been eight days since that stressful and upsetting visit to my mother's house. I'd not spoken to her in eight days, the longest I think we had ever been without speaking to each other, except if one of us was on holiday or something, but never in anger like it is now. She'd reacted so badly to my announcement, called me all sorts of horrible names, and then asked me to leave her house! The emotional pain I'd felt as she spoke to me that way was like a stab direct to my heart. I'd known she might struggle with the idea at first, it being such a massive change, but I'd never expected her to ask me to leave her house, the family home. I thought there would be some room to work with it, get used to it, even to ask me questions about it, but it was clear there was no room for that full stop. My father was just as bad. I'd received a text from him informing me that I had upset my mother ever so much, and not to contact her, or him, or my brothers until I had gotten over my silliness. In all honesty I wasn't so surprised by him, thinking it was silly, or a fad that I could get over, and I wasn't worried by his comments as such, except that they seemed so final. Me and my father had not had the closest parent and offspring relationship over the years, but I had to admit that it did still hurt that this was the end as far as he was concerned unless I stopped what I was doing. But how could I? This wasn't a silliness that I was going to get over, so how was his text anything other than the end of us, the end of me being part of the family. I just didn't know what to do. I mean, was I just meant to walk away from my parents and family like that, and act like I didn't have any, like they were all dead or something? I didn't think my brothers would have reacted so badly, but I didn't know for sure if this was actually the case, that they didn't want anything to do with me, or if my father had told them they couldn't have anything to do with me. They both knew I was golden boy to my mother, were they that low that they saw this as an opportunity to become the new number one. I didn't think either of them were that shallow, but then again, I didn't think my mother would reject me so who knows what my brothers might be thinking. I couldn't risk contacting them now in case this was actually the case, that they didn't want to speak to me. That would be like taking the rejection slap in the face twice, and I couldn't do that to myself again. Not now, not ever.

With everything that was going on in my life right now I was still off sick from work. I just couldn't face going in, I had too much to deal with as it was, and the situation with my mother made it a whole lot worse. It was so unlike me, and I felt like I was letting my colleagues down, but I had to put myself first for once. I'd been rather cowardly too, and had put off telling my girlfriend the news. That was just one challenge too much for me in my current mental state of mind, and after how mum reacted, I was rather unsure about telling people full stop. Maybe I was being weak, or an arse, I didn't know which one, but as it all whirled about inside my head like clothes being tossed about in a tumble dryer I started to cry, the tears hanging from the bottom of my jaw momentarily before dropped off and landing on my jeans. I could have done with a hug, a shoulder, and someone who loved me to tell me it was all going to be okay. It was at that moment that I realised that no one in the world loved me at this moment in time, no one loved the real me. They only loved the person they wanted me to be and were only prepared to love that person, not me. So much for unconditional. It was like starting over again as a human, being born into the world at 32, and having to find loved ones and a new family from scratch. You just don't find family though; this was going to be a tough old lonely ride.

The only thing I had to look forward to now was the late-night appointment with my counsellor that I had booked in a few days ago. I felt relieved that I had something else to focus on other than the rejection from my family. At least my counsellor accepted me, and not just because he was being paid to accept. I'd had also made a big decision concerning the appointment this evening. I had decided to go as me, the new real me, the person who I should be. And I had also decided to drive myself to the surgery, as me. Venturing out in the big wide world was scary, but it was something I needed to do and tackle, to get that first occasion under my belt and out of the way. This seemed like the ideal opportunity. My mother knew now, and my brothers, and I didn't care if any of them saw me out as the new me. It was a situation that had to happen at some point, and after the rejection I felt the other day I really didn't care about being sensitive towards their feelings at the moment. Harsh some may say, but as the days wore on some of my hurt was starting to turn to anger, an easier emotion to handle as far as I was concerned. The only other person who really needed to know now was my girlfriend, and I thought I'd take the risk that she wouldn't be out at that end of town to bump into me. She'd text to say she was staying in after work, if I'd wanted to pop by so there was very little risk I would see her out anyway. I wouldn't be popping by hers tonight though, not yet. Tonight was all about me taking a big step and I wanted to save all my mental energy for me, for once. I would just have to see her another day but being weak I text her back and said I'd see how the evening went. I didn't like myself for giving her hope that I might pop round but what else could I do? Ideally, I didn't want her to change her mind and go out.

I had spent all day trying to keep my mind off my family and keeping myself busy. I had spent hours picking an outfit for my session this evening. It felt like I was getting ready to go out for a drink with friends rather than to talk to a therapist, but that's sort of what it felt like to be honest, a night out. It was my only real genuine social interaction that I had to look forward to at the moment, and I wanted to look my best. I was going somewhere where I could be the real me, I could dress as me and I could talk to someone who wouldn't judge me and end up ignoring me by the end of the night. It was the best night out that was on offer right now, and I planned to fully embrace it. I had also been keeping myself busy online, purchasing lots of nice new things. Ever since my visit to the charity shop I'd wanted to fill the wardrobe up with nice things that I could show off the real me in. It had kept my mind off my parents for the most part, though they did pop into my mind from time to time, I just had to keep pushing them out if I was to stay sane. The result was a full wardrobe of lots of beautiful, classy lady's clothes so I couldn't complain too much, and my old clothes would soon have no use for me at all. The charity shop in town had served a great purpose though, helping me with sizing, but I'd wanted things that I knew I wanted to wear out and be seen in. I would re-donate the clothes I had brought back to the charity shop, along with my man clothes when I was ready.

I'd done quite well all considering, with my on-line ordering. I'd only had one outfit from my deliveries so far that I'd needed to return for a bigger size, which wasn't bad going in my mind. I wasn't ready for an actual face to face shopping experience yet, I wanted to look more like me before I ventured out where I could try things on and not get funny looks. The other thing that had taken my mind off my family this week (a bit) was the arrival of my beautiful wig. Tonight I was going to get the chance to wear it out for the first time and I was so excited by the thought. The hair on it was so smooth, unlike my course short hair. I couldn't stop running my fingers through it, loving the way it felt in my hands. I'd opted for a down style with the wig so that my hair hung over my shoulders. It would allow me, with a slight dip of my head, to move my hair forward and partly cover my face. I had practiced that very move, it would allow me a small hiding place, in case I needed it. I also preferred down hair on people, on women, so it wasn't all about being hidden, though that was probably a heavy influence tonight I had to admit to myself. At the moment I was having to shave my face twice a day too, to try and help keep my face as soft and bristle free as I could. I still didn't know what makeup to put on my face to try and hide the darkness they crept across it, which was a big concern of mine, but I'd been practicing with eye shadow and mascara, both of which were getting their first public outing tonight as well. I wore a longish skirt and another pair of kitten heeled shoes that I'd ordered on line and I clutched a small black handbag into my side as I left the house and walked to my car. None of the neighbours were out in the street as I left the house, making it easy for me, but not wanting to take after my mother and worry what outside people might think I had given myself a good talking too and headed out the door without even checking who was outside first. I had planned that I would just greet them how I usually did, get in the car and drive away, just like any other day. There was no need to explain there and then to them, they didn't own me, but I wasn't given the chance to be that brave, this time. Another day, I'd do that to them another day I told myself as I closed the car door. There would be lots of opportunity, and there was no turning back now.

I reached the surgery in good time and made myself comfortable in the waiting room. I'd just picked up one of the magazines from the table in front of me when I heard a 'Hello' from the counsellor as he greeted me. 'Do come though' He gestured towards his room and then pointed towards the empty chair inviting me to sit down. He seemed a little more rushed this time, but I was a little more paranoid too I guess.

'Firsts things first. Have we decided on a new name yet?' He used the royal we, I guess 'we' meant me and him.

'Only going forward, I don't want to keep calling you Michael, as that is not who you have come as tonight, and that is not who you are anymore is it.' It wasn't asked as a question, was more of a statement 'and I don't want to appear rude.' He finished.

Maybe I'd misinterpreted his rushed demeanour earlier as that was the kindest thing anyone had said to me in days, but that wasn't hard considering my last conversation with anyone face to face had been with my disapproving mother. But still, it brought another tear to my eye as I soaked up his kindness gratefully. Crying seemed to be something that was happening a lot more often to me at the moment. I dried my eyes and finally replied to him.

'No, not yet. I don't have a name yet. Sorry.' I felt annoyed with myself at this, surely this was the basics?? What did I want people to call me. Why hadn't I given this more thought?

'You don't need to apologies. You take as long as you need to decide. It's just some people find it helps them. Once they have their new name it helps them let go and say goodbye to the old them and to start living as the new them. You may find the same.'

'To be honest I have been focussing on my new clothing and telling my parents, I forgot about a new name.' I begin. 'One went well, and the other not so well. I bet you can guess which one went well...' I gestured to my new outfit. We sat for a moment, both in silence, me letting that thought sit, him waiting to see if I had finished speaking. It wasn't for him to banter and joke about such things, even if I did, and he was never one to interrupt. My blasé about it all was all a coping mechanism, I knew that, and so did he.

'M. Can we just call me M for now? 'I asked. 'It means I can ditch Michael, but I don't want to rush into a new name just yet, it has to be right.' I try to justify myself but in all honesty I hadn't given it much thought, and had sort of forgotten I would need to change my name. It's a big thing deciding on a new name, and not something to go about lightly. Our parents just lumber us with a name from birth. Some people come off okay with what they are given and have a cool name, others are not so lucky and spend a life time going by a nick name rather than their own horrendous birth name, but when you actually get to choose what you would like to be called forever, legally, it harder than I'd ever thought it would be.

'Of course, M.' He replied. I smiled in return, which made me feel instantly happier than I'd felt all week.

The rest of the session flew by, and I'd found it all so useful I almost bounced out of the surgery. I now had a whole host of appointments booked in for various things, and my life was all moving in the right direction for change. My therapist had booked me in with a makeup specialist too, after I spoke to him about my concerns on what to use. Apparently it was a lady that worked with the practice a couple of days a week that I would be seeing. She was a makeup professional and worked in various industries, whatever that meant. Whatever her background, I genuinely couldn't wait for that appointment to come around. I felt as excited as a kid about to see Father Christmas. A professional to show me how to apply makeup, and what would be best for me and my skin tone. This was a dream come true as far as I was concerned. I drove home happier than when I had drove to the surgery, almost forgetting I was driving as M, in my kitten heel shoes, and not as Michael, usually in heavy wide boots. I'd had to really focus on my drive to the surgery, getting use to rocking my heel off of the thin kitten heel and I'd struggled to consciously keep my feet steady for driving. The excitement of my makeup appointment seemed to help me forget about the physical side of driving, and when I remembered I realised that it wasn't that bad really, and I didn't need to think about it as much as I had been on the way there. Driving was driving at the end of the day.

I neared my house and pulled into my drive with the biggest grin on my face like I had won the lottery. Amazingly the complete 'down' I had left with now felt like a complete 'up'. I was on an emotional roller-coaster with a long ride ahead of me. I wasn't naive though, I was aware there would be a lot more of the downs, and then some hyperactive ups, before I finally reached the stage that I could stay on a more level and normal feeling. Emotions, you could have a good understanding of how they might work and make you feel, but you still couldn't change them happening to you, even if you tried. You couldn't stop feeling a certain way just like that, no matter how well informed you were, or how hard you tried to beat what was going on inside. And I couldn't stop the feeling I had of a super 'up' or a 'high' as some might call it, which all came crashing down to a heart in mouth moment as I opened my car door. My stomach felt like it had dropped out of me as I opened my car door, my right leg moving out of the car complete with a kitten heel shoe attached to my foot as I then looked up into the eyes of my next-door neighbour. Gulp. I must go for this; I can't hide now. I step out the car, straighten my skirt which had risen during the drive, held my head high, and said 'hello'.

MIA, 24TH JULY 5AM

I hadn't gotten much sleep last night, and when I had finally drifted off, I'd been very restless for the rest of the night, flitting between that sleep and half sleep that plagues us all at some point in our lives. I didn't feel rested at all, and why would I, I should still be asleep now. I didn't know if it was the alcohol in my system, or the feeling I'd been left with at the end of my date the night before, but I just couldn't shake the feeling and switch off. It was probably a mixture of both things playing their part in keeping me awake. I'd found that before, an alcohol fuelled sleep was the worst sleep you could have, so much so you might as well not even bother closing your eyes. But this did feel a bit different to just a hangover alone. I felt so unsettled somehow, like a mini panic attack was swelling within, and I recognised the emotion in myself as something that was a little bit irrational. I had no concrete fact that anything in my life right now was not as it seemed at face value. I needed to knock it on the head and give myself a mental slap around the face, and a break. I needed to stop being so hard on myself all the time. I decided to get out of bed. I wasn't going back to sleep now so I went downstairs and put the kettle on to make a strong coffee. I saw my laptop sat there, inviting me, in, I gave in, and turned it on. There was only one person I could talk to in times like this, but I didn't want to disturb him at this unearthly hour with a text or phone call, that was above and beyond the call of duty, but I could sit here and send him an e-mail instead.

Powered by the caffeine in my coffee as it surged around my body I began to offload my feeling onto the screen in front of me. There must have been steam coming from my fingertips as they hit the keyboard where I was typing so fast, wanting to get it all down and out of my system. I loved an email chat, where if I said something wrong I could just hit delate and start again, making sure everything was in the right order and that it all made sense before I hit 'send'. It felt good to get it out there in the world and out of my head. After giving my good friend the usual 'hello how are you' polite conversational openers I began with a rundown of the night's events. I could just get straight to the point I wanted to talk about with him. That's just how it was with us.

'You see, I just don't get it, why he didn't want to stay over with me? Am I expecting too much? Am I placing emotions on him that I am feeling, but he might not be feeling them yet?'

Even typing that last sentence out in black and white helped me rationalise a bit. It made me think, made me see what should have been obvious. Just because I might be head over heels falling for him, and he was all I could think about day and night, it didn't mean that he was in that same place as me yet. He might be getting there, just a little slower than I was. He might like me, a lot, but maybe had stuff in his past that he didn't want to share with me yet that was holding him back a little too. I hadn't even considered that he might have stuff going on. I realised then just how selfish I was being. But I still carried on, I had stuff I needed to get off my chest.

'Now we both know I have been around the block a few times, but I have never felt this way before, as we know, and it's totally knocked me for six in all honesty. I don't know if I even like feeling like this! Crazy yeah? I seem to have lost all sense of the direction I was going in life, but that's mad, as surly this is the feeling I was working towards and looking for my whole life, right? I mean, it's taken a couple of years really, and I knew it would be different now, but I didn't realise how different my feelings and emotions would be, and how hidden I have been within myself for all these years. I don't know if this is normal either or if there is even a normal out there. I know there is nothing you can do to fix it, I'm not asking you to do that, I know I must do that for myself. But you know I have always valued your opinion, so, any words of wisdom for me? MX'

Our relationship was a funny one, having begun professionally, to a degree, for one of us at least. But even on our first meeting we seemed to hit is off as friends too, in a weird way. Nothing romantic, and nothing was ever said, that would have been too odd for both of us, I think. He wasn't my 'type' like that so there was never anything there from me, nor from him to me, he knew too much for a start. But sometimes in life you meet someone and there's just something between you, and sometimes it's an instant thing you can't put a word on to describe it. There had always been a fondness between us, and at one point I'd have considered him to be my best friend, and I probably still do in many respects. The downside of it all was it always made it hard for me to work out where our boundaries really were, and how far I could take it when talking to him, with the support seeking, as that wasn't why we'd stayed friends beyond our professional meet ups. I decided it would go one of two ways with my e-mail. He'd either read it and take note of the time it was sent and ignore it, putting it down to a drunken e-mail that I hadn't really intended to send (as had happened on more than one occasion in the past), or I'd get some pearls of wisdom back putting me right in my place, where I needed to be put. I didn't expect a call, but you never know. If he did or didn't come back with anything though, what with it being a Saturday morning, 5:45am now, I didn't want to sit staring at the screen waiting for a reply as I knew I'd be in for a long wait. The typing had had a good effect, it has made me tired, thank goodness, and it was a proper tiredness now, one I wanted to enjoy. I headed back up to bed, I was asleep before my head even hit the pillow.

It was noon before I woke up again, my eyes lifting slowly, blinking against the sunlight streaming through the gap in my curtains, a momentary feeling of relaxed lightness encased my body. Then my mind began to join the awake world, its pistons firing up and engaging in thinking and remembering. My mind wanted to get out of bed and go and turn the laptop on to check for any replies I might have received. My body resisted for ten more minutes, trying to hold onto that peaceful feeling, it wasn't a feeling I got to experience much, and I was rather enjoying the moment. In the end my active mind got the better of me and forced me out of bed and downstairs. I fired the laptop up whilst the kettle boiled. I could sense it was going to be one of those caffeine intensive days. I logged onto my email account to see what had come in during the last few hours. There was a flurry of the usual spam, filling my screen as my inbox updated itself. Then I spotted the one I hoped might appear, one from my friend. I held my cursor over it, hoping he wasn't going to give me what for. But then why would he...? I double clicked to open the mail and began to read with my coffee cup in my hand.

'Your feelings are perfectly normal Mia, but you need to tell him the truth, otherwise these feelings are a waste of time, as is your worry. You know I'm right x'

And that was it, short, sweet and to the point. Nothing more, nothing less. Not even any feedback on how his day had been, how life was going for him. He was to the point, but then again that's the way he was, and deep down that's the way I liked people to be. I have to admit I was slightly put out by his reply though, but only because I knew he was right, and I knew I should have told my new date the truth sooner. I should have been honest from the start and I don't know why I wasn't really. Now I was in too deep and so emotionally involved and emotionally invested that it was hard to tell him the truth and for it all be okay. And the pain if he, my new man, didn't like the truth and walked away from it all, well, I just don't know how I would pick myself up from that now. We, me and my best friend, had spoken about that very subject at length before, on more than one occasion, before I'd even started looking for a love, before I even had any emotions for someone, so this was no surprise to me really, but yet in an odd way it was a surprise. It's easy to talk about being truthful, so easy, but to put it into action is another thing altogether. I paused over the keyboard, I needed to send a reply and acknowledge that I understood what he was saying to me, and that I was okay with that, but I didn't know what or how to say that, as I don't really know how I feel right now. In the end I went with 'I know, sorry I think I was a tad tired. See you down the club house Wednesday I believe?' Totally evasive, totally the old me, and totally a load of crap. I was not happy with myself. On the plus side I did have until Wednesday to pull myself back together. We'd gotten into the habit of meeting up once a month for a social catch up, and I didn't want my friend to be dreading our next meet up and thinking it was going to be a free therapy session, I needed to be the strong me I had grown to like when I walked into the club on Wednesday. My friend needed his downtime too, I realised that, and I didn't want to be the one to ruin his night out. I needed to 'woman up' and sort my shit out.

MICHAEL, 31ST JULY 3PM

It had been two days since I had encountered my neighbours as the new me, the real me. My neighbour had been surprisingly middle of the road about our encounter, which had surprised me in a way. I'd made the first move and said 'hello, how are you?' to which he'd responded with a polite 'Hello, fine thanks.' He'd not returned the question though, which he normally would have, and I suspect by the look on his face he was perhaps jumping to some conclusions about me that would be along the right lines, but I knew he wouldn't be totally right with his thoughts, how could he, I know I wasn't main stream at the moment. On reflection maybe didn't want to hear the answer to 'how are you?' as he could see I was confused, or he may have just been too shocked to ask, I didn't know, and actually I didn't care. I'd just jumped over a massive hurdle for me, and that was all that really mattered about our encounter in my mind. He was a nice bloke though, honest, had the standard 9-5 job, wife, 2 kids, and took a holiday once a year. I was probably a bit too 'way out there' at the moment for the regular life he had built around himself. We'd both paused, just looking at each other, the silence expanding between us, neither one wanting to make the next move. To be honest I didn't know what the next move should be. Then he came too, and broke the awkwardness for us both with 'John at number 24 is having a neighbour's BBQ next Sunday, if you are free? He asked me to tell you about it as he hasn't got your phone number and he is away until the Friday before. He thought it would be nice for us all to get together. It's been a while.'

'Oh, Okay, thanks for letting me know, I'll check my dairy. I can't think that I'm doing anything. It would be good to catch up with everyone.'

And with that he went on his way to continue his normal day, and I locked my car and went into my house to continue my version of a normal day at the moment. I suspect he went straight indoors and told his wife what he had just seen, like you would, and I'd gone in and sat on the stairs in disbelief at how normal the conversation had turned out.

So now I was two days down the line from the encounter and I'd not seen anyone since then face to face. That was my own fault though as I'd locked myself in the house for the last two days giving myself some serious thinking time. Todays was a good day though; I was about to go for my first session with the makeup lady. I was so excited about the appointment and learning what I needed to do to make myself look like how I wanted, but the occasion had sort of been dampened by my neighbours invite to the BBQ. I hadn't even considered that people would invite me out to social events at the moment, and it has thrown me a little. I'll admit, I'm so self-absorbed with all my stuff that I'd sort of forgotten that the big world still rumbles on around me. My problem with it is, my neighbour has invited Michael to a BBQ, and not me, and I don't know what I should do. Half of me wants to not bother going at all and to just hide away from it all, lie, pretend I am already going elsewhere, the other half of me wants to go and face the music and get it over and done with and face them all in one hit, as me. They would have to get use to the real me eventually, I was still their neighbour after all, and living in the same neighbourhood with them. This wasn't going to go away.

I arrived at my appointment half an hour early and took a seat in the waiting room. I always arrived early, I had a fear of being late and missing something, so I always allowed lots of time. A lady came and sat near me and introduced herself as Anna. She seemed very nice, and very confident.

'What stage are you at?' She asked as she made herself comfortable on the chair opposite me. It wasn't what I was expecting to be asked, and I stumbled a little with my answer.

'Early stages. I'm seeing the makeup specialist today.' I offered.

'Have you started with your hormone therapy yet?'

I tried not to take offence at her direct approach, especially given the setting but I was a bit taken back. She was one of those instantly likable out there characters, bold, says whatever pops into her mind with no elaborate build up, and I imagine she was just the same wherever she was with whoever she was talking to.

'No, not yet, I'm seeing someone about that next week.' I responded. I started to feel relaxed in her company. I liked her approach, there was probably a lot I could learn from her.

'Best thing you'll ever do, totally changes everything. And you'll wonder why you took so long to get here. I've got my final surgery in two weeks, I'm counting the days, I can't wait. It's been a long two years for me.' She smiled.

'Wow' was all I could offer her in response. The enormity of the change and challenges ahead for me finally hitting home. This wasn't going to be fixed overnight, and I had a lot of hurdles to jump over first. My mind was about to blow with it all. I wanted to ask her a million questions about how she felt, how she found stuff, and how she kept sane with it all but before we could go any further my name was called out by a member of staff. I stood up and started to make my way over to the lady who had called me, I presume she was the makeup lady. I paused and turned back to Anna.

'I hope it all goes well for you in a couple of weeks Anna. I hope to see you again.' As I genuinely did. I think Anna would be someone I could talk quite openly too. I wouldn't need to hold back talking about my fears, and telling the truth, I could see she didn't do 'holding back'. I think I needed to be more like Anna. She raised a hand to wave me off and gave me a gentle smile. The encounter left me with a lot of questions, and no answers.

The makeup lady sat me in a comfortable upright chair with a big mirror on the table in front of me. It was a small room but somehow felt airy and cosy all that the same time. I felt at ease in this room, I liked it. The lady spun my chair round so that I was facing her. She was sat on a tall stool, I guess so she could be sat at a comfortable height to work on my face. This was a whole new world for me, as were most things at the moment. The lady introduced herself as Sarah and gave me a brief rundown on her makeup experience to date. I hadn't thought that her CV would matter to me before I came here, but as she started to rattle off the long list of her exceptional work, including working on set doing makeup for films, I have to admit I was rather impressed by her and her knowledge of the subject. It resulted in making me feel a whole lot more confident in her ability to be able to cover up Michael and bring out the real me. I was glad she had taken the time to give me her history now.

I'd been half attempting to apply a few products myself over the last few weeks, but I realised pretty quickly into our lesson that I'd been doing it all very wrong. I'd grown up with brothers which probably hadn't helped as I'd never really been exposed to the complications of creating beauty. Layers was the way forward, it seemed. A layer of primer, a layer of foundation, a layer of face powder, all building up to try and cover the dark patches on my skin that years of shaving had left behind. I hated the fact that I still had to shave, I was looking forward to the day

I could stop tormenting my face with shape blades scaping at my skin, making it as tough as old boots. I tried to focus on what she was showing me, as I knew with the way my face hair grew, and for the time being this process would need to be a twice a day application, especially if I was going to go out again in the evening. It wouldn't matter so much if I was staying in, but then again maybe it should matter to me from now, every day twice a day, don't let Michael shine though even for one evening. I needed to get myself into the habit of wearing makeup at all times, just until my face was a little less Michael at least.

As the makeup session progressed, I was so impressed with the coverage on my face, and how Sarah was making me look. I almost didn't recognise myself when I risked a full look at myself in the mirror. The gentle way she'd applied my eye liner gave such beautiful results, my eyes looked totally different to the ones that had been looking back at me, all sad and lifeless, for so many years. These new eyes were wide, bright and very happy. I realised though I'd been very heavy handed with my previous attempts on my eye makeup and had drawn far too thick a black line on the edge of my eye. The eyes Sarah had given me were delicate, and the prettiest I'd ever seen.

When I had been looking at makeup on line I'd been so tempted with heavy bold colours, thinking that would be the only way to cover and hide Michael from the world. I'm so glad now I didn't waste a host of money on stuff I wouldn't now use. Sarah had chosen much softer colours for me to match my natural toning, and the results were out of this world, in my mind. I almost couldn't see Michael at all behind the gentle colours and tones. A tear spring to my eye, again, as I took in the new me, from the outside. Up to now I'd only ever known me from the inside, but here I was, emerging from the dark depths of manhood into a light world of womanhood.

'Don't cry sweetie.' Sarah said as she took a tissue from the box on the side and gently dabbed away my tear for me. 'You'll ruin your makeup.' She smiled, clearly trying to lift my mood.

'It's a happy tear.' I assured her with a smile.

'I know it is honey.' She said. 'I've seen many a happy tear in this room before believe me. This is you.' She pointed at my reflection in the mirror. 'And you've been waiting a while to meet you I bet.' She was so gentle and caring, and that was the kindest moment with another human I'd had in a long while. I felt like she really did care about me, and this wasn't just a job to her.

Sarah spent a bit more time running through some other makeup options for me, for different types of occasions. Day time and night time required difference applications, colours and tones it seems, something I'd not really given much thought to before, I thought it would all be the same. She also showed me how to clean the makeup from my face properly too, as that was just as important I learnt. Good old soap and water were not going to cut it for me anymore. Sarah then got me to re-apply my makeup and replicate what she had done earlier, all under her watchful eye and guidance. I was a little unsteady with some of the application methods, it was hard doing it all in reverse looking at yourself in the mirror, but Sarah was there to help and show me with gentle reminders. I could tell she wanted me to walk out of here looking amazing and having done it all myself. Nothing seemed too much trouble for her either, I felt so happy in her company. It was almost like she was an instant friend, and I had known her for years. I had to remind myself she was a paid for professional and that she wasn't my friend, no matter how much I might want her to be. Maybe I was just desperate for a friend, I felt like this about Anna earlier. But I desperately wanted to talk to her about my feelings and things that were on my mind, I wanted to ask for her opinion on this BBQ that I had been invited to, like friends would ask each other. I wanted to hear what she would suggest I do. Should I go, or not go at all.

And if I do go, should I go as the real me, or carry on hiding from the world for a bit longer, until I was more woman than man. It was all so unknown and confusing, and how could she give an objective answer when she didn't really know me, that would be unfair of me to ask. I realised she was a trained makeup artist, and not a therapist, but she just seemed like she would know the right thing to do anyway. I tried to hold back, but the more I thought about it, the harder it was to stop the tears from building up inside and start flowing again.

'Are you sure you are okay sweetie?' She asked 'Or is this all a little too much too soon for you? We can stop if you like, try again another day?'

'Oh no, please don't. I love what you have done with me, I look amazing. I'm just thinking of all the wasted years I've had, that's all.'

'I do understand. But are you sure that's all? I can get someone to come in if you need?'

I didn't want anyone else from the practice coming in, that all seemed a little over the top and melodramatic, but I did take her last question as an invitation to perhaps say a little bit more and expand on my thoughts. So, I did what I had been trying to stop myself doing with her, I opened up.

'It's just I've been invited to a BBQ by my neighbour, for like a neighbours gathering, and I just don't know who I should go as. This is all still so new to me. I've not told many people yet about me yet, and I just don't know what the right thing to do is, for everyone, not just for me.' I explained. She wheeled her stool in closer to me and cupped my face in her hands, an action that surprised me a little. I'd never felt such comfort from a human being before.

'Sweetie.' She started. 'You might still mechanically be Michael, at the moment, but that will change in time. You are M, in here' she squeezed my face in-between her hands 'and that is who you should go as, no question about it. You are also M on the outside now too. Look at you, you are a beautiful woman.' We both looked at my reflection in the mirror. I wasn't convinced about the beautiful bit as an overall appearance, there was still a way to go even with fabulous makeup, but I did like my eyes. She was right about one thing though, about needing to go to the BBQ as me. I'd put other people's feelings first for my entire life, it was time to start putting myself first for a change. Her kindness made me feel I was crazy to even have considered going as anyone else other than M, as me, as a woman. No matter what the outcome was, or what people felt about it, they would just have to get over it and get used to it. And if they didn't, so be it, just like my parents. And I would just have to deal with people's reactions too, as the alternative was not an option anymore.

MICHAEL, 2ND AUGUST 3PM

Today was the day, it was here, my big 'outing' across the road. It was an 'outing' in more ways than one. Today was BBQ day, and I was as nervous about it as hell. I had got my head around the fact that I would be going as M, facing my fears, and getting on with my life. It was the only way, I had to do it and I had to stop hiding behind the lovable Michael. I also had to prove I could live as a woman if I was to take this change any further, and that didn't include being selective about when I appeared as a women or played safe as a man. And I was a woman, there was no choice about that. If I didn't, the hospital and the people who make the decisions on these things wouldn't consider me for the operation, and I didn't want to live in this half world I was stuck in any longer, even if it was the easier option at times. At the back of my mind I knew I still needed to arrange to meet up with her, my lady friend, but that could wait for now, or for today at least. Maybe in a few days' time perhaps. It was all too much for me, it was like I could only deal with one challenging situation at a time, and the wimp in me was sort of hoping that she might get the hint and not bother with me anymore and just float away, like many before her had. Then there was the selfish side of me, the side that will really miss her, as I found her such a positive person, and genuinely enjoyed her company. I sort of wanted to talk to her about it all, this crazy world my head was stuck in, but as a friend only, for support, but to even stand a chance of that happening I needed to tell her the truth about me first. There were parts of me I didn't like much right now, and that's a hard place to be with yourself. It was both external bits of me, which I was hoping the doctors could change, and there were some internal parts about my personality of late that I wasn't too keen on either. Try as I might, I couldn't change my thought processes, even though they were disappointing in my treatment of people to say the least. I just needed to try and get on with me, the way I was right now. I might need me soon enough as I might be the only one around left to talk to if it didn't go too well when I told my girlfriend about what had been going on with me. I'd already lost my parents, and clearly my brothers and the rest of my family along with them. I might be adding the neighbours to that list shortly too, depending on how it goes this afternoon.

I stood in front of my new wardrobe scanning my skirts and dresses, trying to decide on what outfit to wear this afternoon. I didn't want to be too in their faces with it, with me, and obvious looking, or even look like a bad trannie as I had heard one lady at the practice describing herself when she first tackled her change. I didn't want to give any of the kids in the neighbourhood an excuse to stare at me too much either. And knowing what kids could be like that could be a tough one, kids being the toughest audience of all in any life situation. It was a hard thing to achieve, this balance, ticking all of the right boxes, wearing the right thing. I pulled out a pair of white knee length shorts and thought they were better than a skirt, on this occasion anyway. I grabbed a pair of sparkly flip flips and tried them on together. My toe nails were painted a rosy pink colour which I loved, though my feet still looked manly to me. I changed my mind on the footwear for now and grabbed a nice pair of pumps I had brought myself recently. They were a light colour to go with the shorts and would work in a garden setting better too. Now for a top. I looked through my rails again, I had brought so much recently it was a little indulgent even by my standards. My hand rested on a nice loose-fitting pink top I had brought just the other day. I liked pink, and if I couldn't show off my bright toe nails then a pink top would have to be my splash of colour instead.

I didn't yet have a bust of my own to show off, that was all still very flat and manly looking, but the feminine shape was something that I was working towards. It would take a while for me to have my very own set of real boobs that I could be proud of, I knew that. Firstly I would need to go through hormone therapy, and then see how that changed my shape and what I could grew myself. If that wasn't enough for me I would then be left with the decision if I went down the breast implant route. That all took time, and I needed something more instant to help me feel better about myself and help me look like a woman. As a stop gap I had brought myself a bra, on-line of course! I'd done some extensive googling about how to measure myself, and what that would equate to in a bra size. I didn't know yet if got it all right, but I'd felt quite girly doing it. In the end I'd gone for a cup size that I thought I would like to be by the end of it all. Sadly, it had not arrived yet, the downside of internet shopping, nothing was instantly with you. I'd got a bit carried away at the time and had bitten the bullet and ordered a pair of breast prosthesis too. I thought they might help give me that womanly shape. I'd found them on line, I never knew you could buy stuff like that before. I think they were primarily for breast cancer patients, but I thought they might be good to try. I'd thought that as well as shape, they might help me get use to the feel and weight of having breasts. There was still so much to learn! I wanted people to take me seriously as a woman, but I realised that I sometimes still looked like a man dressed up in woman's clothes. I had to pick my outfits carefully for venturing outside, especially for now.

I dressed in the outfit I had picked for the BBQ, and with my wig on and in place I didn't think I looked too bad. I'd toned down my make up too and just went with discrete and natural looking, as it was only an afternoon BBQ. I had put into practice what Sarah had taught me when I did my makeup, less is best. I didn't know if she said that to everyone, or just me, after I'd shown her a picture of my first heavy handed attempt at makeup. I took another look at myself in the mirror, just to make sure I was passable, as a woman. I was keen to get over to the BBQ now. I wanted to be one of the first to arrive, so the other neighbours would arrive to me, rather than me arriving to them and making a grand ta-dah type entrance, if that made sense. It's what made me comfortable, whether I was doing it the right or wrong way I wasn't sure. I didn't have anyone to run it by anymore, or even a friend I could have brought along with me, so I had to go with my gut instinct on this, and crack on with it.

I left the house and made myself hold my head up high as I made the short walk across our quiet road over to my neighbour's house. I was glad I opted for pumps in the end, I think it might make walking around his garden on the grass a little easier, and as I strode across the shot walk I felt more confident about my footwear decision. Although I did crave my new heels, I felt they defined womanhood somehow. But my blinkered jealous life vision of woman always being able to wear sexy heels was fast diminishing. They just weren't always practical, even for the most sexist of woman, pumps and flats still had a place in every woman's wardrobe.

My finger lingered over the doorbell, a moment's hesitation letting a seed of doubt creep back in. I forced myself to push the bell button down releasing the familiar 'ding dong' that was my neighbours eccentric doorbell chime. I waited for what felt like an age for someone to come to the door and welcome me in. I hoped it would be one of the adults, and not one of the kids. I could see through their glass panel on the door that my worst fear was about to come true. One of their little boys came padding down the hallway to the door to let me in. I racked my brain to remember his name. I should remember it, considering the number of times he had played football in my back garden. My brain was just so fussy lately. Just in time his name came to me as he opened the door with his beaming child face.

'Hi Mr Cook.' He stood there without batting an eye at me, he just smiled, as he always did. He was a very polite child, about 10 years old and always happy. He was one kid that was really embracing being a kid and would have the best memories of it all when he was older. You never heard him moaning or complaining about anything, he just got on and enjoyed his life. I hoped for his sake he managed to hold onto that attitude through the trauma of puberty.

'Hi Brad. Can I come in?' I asked. He stepped back from the door and walked back down the hall, leaving me to close the door behind us and follow him into their house.

'MUM...' He called out loudly, as only kids do, not waiting until they are in the same room as the person they are talking to. 'MR COOK IS HERE..' then he turned to me and said, 'All the adults are in the garden, you can go and find them there.' As he scooted off back into the living room. I peeked my head in as I walked by and could see a computer game had been paused mid battle. His brother was sat patiently waiting for him to return so they could continue their game and fight. I left them to it and headed to the patio doors where I could see my neighbour trying to fire up the BBQ. Something struck me as a 'thought worth noting' as I walked through the kitchen into the garden in a slight daze. I clearly still looked like Michael, like a man, as Brad had called me Mr Cook, but little Brad hadn't been fazed at all by my more feminine outfit or makeup. It might have helped I wasn't in a skirt, but I was wearing a woman's pink top, and more importantly I was wearing a wig! Brad hadn't batted an eye lid to any of it, he just took it all in his stride and accepted me as me, I think. I was encouraged by our encounter. Maybe kids were more accepting of things than I gave them credit for. Some kids anyway. Now for the adults.

I stepped out of the house onto the patio and said hello to the few people who had already arrived. It wasn't the full group, but it was more people than I had hoped for at this early stage of the afternoon. I held my breath and waited for a response. My neighbour finally looked up from his BBQ issues.

'Hi Mike. Grab yourself a beer.' He pointed towards a table where beer and wine had been laid on for us. He always shortened my name, my old name, to Mike. I hadn't minded his familiarity in the past, even though he was the only person I knew who shortened my name, and it didn't bother me too much today either to be fair. He didn't know the full story and probably just assumed I was still Mike as I hadn't yet told him otherwise.

'Thanks. I'll grab one in a minute. Did you want a hand with that?' I asked pointing at the BBQ and the unlit coals.

'Got it all in hand mate.' He responded. 'Plus, wouldn't want you to dirty your outfit.' He finished off with a wink. I didn't know how to take that statement. Was that his way of showing acceptance? Or was that disapproval? Or was that just plain old banter? I was so confused I just didn't know how to take what he had said. I took a deep breath and decided to go with acceptance. Anything else would have me running for the door, running across the road back to my house where I could just hide away from everyone. I knew I couldn't do that, not after getting this far across the road, and that wasn't just the tarmac road that separated our houses. Maintaining my composure, I walked over to the table and poured myself a glass of white wine. Bottles of beer were not very lady like to hold, and I wanted to try my best to carry off feminine this afternoon, even though I was still hauling this manly bulk of a body about.

In the end not that many more people came to the BBQ, maybe as it had been a bit short notice, maybe they all had other plans. But that didn't matter as it was turning out to be one of those really nice relaxing afternoons and I'm so glad I came along to it. It wasn't just about getting out the house as M, showing the world who I am, but more about just enjoying other people's company on a nice sunny afternoon, just as people. Man, woman, child, it didn't really matter at the end of the day, when you boiled it down like that. The conversations around the garden were all middle of the road, to a point, and our hosts were nothing but pleasant, and I couldn't complain about that. It was nice because it had been a while since I had held a nice middle of the road conversation with anybody, and I had been missing this in my life since I had told my parents about me. A conversation with no consequence or real purpose. I could feel people looking at me the whole time though, their gaze wanting to ask a million questions, but the words not brave enough to leave their mouths for fear of the answer. I would have to get use to that feeling, and maybe in time I would. At the end of the day these were nice honest people who were not going to be rude to me after inviting me into their home. They hadn't asked me to leave as I was breaking the mould of normal, and were happy to entertain me in their home, unlike my own family. When I finally left their garden a few hours later, well fed and with several wines sloshing around inside me, it wasn't with a heavy heart or sadness, but with a realisation that life might not be as easy as I thought it might be, as the new me, but that there were people in my life who would accept me however I represented myself, and I could still have a life. I didn't need to hide away like I was dirty or ill anymore, I could come out from behind the darkness.

MIA, 27TH JULY 8PM

Wednesday finally arrived and I was trying to convince myself that I was feeling stronger than I knew I really was. I hadn't heard from him at all, but he had said he was finishing a big project off at work and would be busy with that. I had sort of convinced myself that this was the case and that I just needed to give him that head space he needed to work and to finish the project. And then we would get to spend some time together. I didn't want my mind to spiral out of emotional control, which it sometimes had a tendency to do, and end up a complete mess. It had taken a lot of effort to pull myself back together and get ready to go out tonight for a catch up with my one sort of friend, I didn't want to fall apart now. Over the last few days I had come to the conclusion that life was never just black and white. There were many shadings in the middle that all swirled around to make several grey areas that represented the world around us. I was feeling good about myself and my body, even if parts of my mind weren't playing ball with me. I wanted my friend to see that positivity oozing out of me, I didn't want him to see the lady who sent that pathetic e-mail a few days ago. That wasn't who I wanted to be, and no one wanted to meet up with sad people all the time, especially on one's day off! Where was the fun in that? We all have our own internal battles, sometimes it does you good to park your woes at the door and take time to ask someone else how their life was going. And I decided that tonight I would do just that. Tonight would not be about me for once.

There weren't that many people in the club house tonight, but then we had arrived later than most as we hadn't played the round of golf that they had all enjoyed during the day. Most of the members were retired gentlemen with the odd woman or two thrown into the equation who had taken to the sport. They would play a round of golf in the early afternoon and follow that up with an early dinner in the club house before they then made their way home to their families. Sometimes we'd manage to get a day off work and join them all for a round, sometimes we'd both come straight from work and join them all for dinner and a catch up, but tonight we just went for a drink and most of the people we knew had already left. They were all nice people, and a very accepting group. There was no stress here, no explaining, it was all very laid back, and just what I had needed when we first joined the club. I presume all the people here think we are a couple, though we didn't behave like we are so perhaps that's just an assumption on my part. We've never encouraged that line of thought, but we don't stop it either, as neither of us want them all thinking we are having an affair. It was all a bit odd, but it worked and we always had a nice time here.

I walked over to the bar, the barman was already preparing my G&T, and a coke for Jeremy, my friend. Our drinks order was as predictable as ever. He was a nice barman though, always friendly, never intrusive, he had the right balance for his job. I took our drinks over to our table and sat down. By the look on Jeremys face I could see he was bracing himself for me to refer to my e-mail a few days earlier, but I could also see something much deeper, much sadder, which was very unlike him

'So... how's things?' I asked as I handed him his coke.

'Busy, you know.' He half-heartedly responded. 'You?' He asked the return question; I wasn't sure if I saw a look of dread make its way across his face as he waited for my response to hit him.

'I'm good, thanks Jeremy.' I replied. The conversation had never been this stilted between us, not even on the day we met. The silence started to stretch out between us as the minutes ticked by, I didn't know what to do. I took a sip of my G&T and said 'I'm sorry Jeremy. I shouldn't have emailed you the other night.' It was the only thing I could think was causing the awkwardness between us, and I wanted things to go back to being easy and nice.

He looked at me a little bit surprised. 'You silly woman, you can mail me whenever you like, you know that!' He took a gulp from his glass of coke, not making eye contact with me. 'She's left me Mia. She's packed her bags and gone.' He eyes glazed over, not seeing the room before him anymore, instead looking out at a faraway place only his heart knew where. By 'she' I knew he must mean his wife. I put my hand on his as a gesture of comfort. His skin had a familiar feel, but the scenario was the wrong way round. I was more use to receiving comfort than giving it out. I realised I didn't know what to say to him though. *'I'm sure she'll come back'* wasn't going to work, I didn't know the woman so how would I know that?! *'Have you tired to call her?'* Wasn't going to cut it either, as he obviously would have tried that. Then out of my mouth popped the word 'Why?' before I could stop myself.

He turned to me, seeing me for the first time all evening and said 'don't know, not really.' He went back to thinking but I let the silence fill the space without awkwardness this time. My mind referred back to my sessions when I was the one needing to talk, and how Jeremy had left me time to think, in between his talking. I wanted to offer him the same head space, as best as I could anyway.

'She said my work is me, and she just can't take it anymore. She wants to be with someone who has time for her. Time for them to do stuff together. She doesn't want to 'just exist', in her words. I thought she was happy, I thought we was enjoying life together' He left my hand resting on his, I could see he was enjoying the physical contact, bringing him some comfort at this stressful time.

'Has she already met someone else then?' I asked. The question was out there again before I could stop my mouth.

'Yes, she has. There's no going back now as far as she is concerned, before you ask.'

I raised my other hand to my mouth, in disbelief. From the outside, from the little I knew of Jeremy's family life, everything had seemed so perfect and ideal. A life everyone else strove towards achieving. The house, the kids, the wife not needing to work, all of that stuff people seem to want, yet it appeared that one party wanted more, wanted a love she didn't feel she was getting. There wasn't anything more I could say really to help or change things for him. There was no operation I could offer him that would fix it, there was no pill I could prescribe him either. I didn't even know what to say to him, without making it worse. I felt a little bit out of my depth, having been wrapped up in me for so long offering comfort felt unnatural. Had I really lost the ability to help others I asked myself, how sad. I pushed my G&T glass towards him instead, the only comfort I could think might help.

'Here, have this, I'll drive your car home for you tonight.' He looked at me, took my glass from me and downed the rest of my drink in one go. I'd never seen him do that, usually such a refrained and measured character. I went to the bar and ordered him another G&T, not bothering to ask if he wanted a different drink.

'When did she leave Jeremy?' I asked as I placed his drink down in front of him.

'Two weeks ago.' He responded with a sadness in his eyes.

'Why didn't you say sooner, call me, come and see me, drop me an e-mail. I'd have been here for you!' I felt hurt and so utterly and totally selfish. I had sought help from him during the last two weeks, during one of the most stressful times of his life for him, when he was alone, and sad and confused I had demanded his attention. He had been typical Jeremy and had responded, offering me help during that time. He had sent me kind words to motivate me, and not because he had to, he had wanted to, that much I do know about him. And during all the time he was going through his own hell. Why had I not picked up on something in his e-mail to me, why couldn't I have seen that he needed me more than I needed him for once. Was I that blinded by my own problems, which seemed so insignificant right now? Was I really that selfish? I thought for a moment, not liking the answer I had to give myself. Yes I really was, and that didn't make me a very nice person right now. And even thinking along these lines is kind of selfish in itself. It was time to stop being poor old me, the world is against me. I pushed all my own stress and worry to the back of my mind, closed the door on it, for now. It was time to help the man that had changed my life, it was time to pay him back for everything he had done for me. Nothing else seemed to matter as I looked at him, dejected, sad, lonely. One human to another, my friend was in pain, and I wanted to make that pain go away.

MIA, 29TH JULY 6AM

The last few days had flown by. I hadn't had time to stop and worry about myself, or to even care about anything that was going on in my life right now. I had been staying with Jeremy at his house since Wednesday night. Jeremy had called in sick to work on Thursday, so I had done the same. Staying home on his own was not going to do him any good, he was in a worse place than I thought and I hadn't wanted him rattling around this big house on his own tormenting himself even more. His wife had taken the kids with her, and his once noisy family home was now very quiet and still. I was used to quiet, and a still house, I quite liked it at times, but if you had never had that in your life it must feel weird. I realised Jeremy had just landed in a very lonely place.

This morning, for the first time since I'd arrived at Jeremy's on Wednesday, he seemed to be calming down. He'd stopped crying, which was good, and he was currently eating a slice of toast that I had made for him. It had been like flood gates opening up with him, years and years of being the strong one and holding back personal emotions had all come out in one go. If I was honest, I'd been a little overwhelmed by it and I didn't know how to handle it or him. I didn't know what to say to him without making it worse, but my caring female side had kicked in and I just held him close to me and let him let it all out. Let him talk if he wanted to, or just sit with me in silence if he preferred. I think it helped him, I know it was all that I had wanted at times in the past, just to be held close to someone, no words necessary. When you are at the height of that emotional rollercoaster sometimes it's all you need to keep you grounded. I took the opportunity of this calmer moment to look at my phone. I hadn't had the chance to look at in days, the habit easily dropped when there is something more pressing in your life. I had forgotten my panic of my new man not texting me. I had forgotten the way we had left things the other night and all the confusion and anxiety it had caused me at the time had faded into a more distant memory that it was. I glanced down at the blank screen, not really caring that there was nothing for me to look at. Then I realised the battery had died, so there would be nothing for me to look at. I put the phone back in my bag. For the first time in weeks I wasn't in a mad rush to find a charger either, I'd have to head home later anyway so I could charge it back up then. I really needed a change of clothes and a nice hot shower more than I needed a text message from anyone. Funny how someone else's sad situation can change your perspective on your own problems, or non-problems as they really are in the grand scheme of things. In the cold light of day, and with time to reflect, I had come to the conclusion that I had been rather childish about it all. And when I considered all the things I had dealt with in my life over the last few years and all the things that I had come out the other side of, to then thrown my toys out the pram over something so petty was quite embarrassing even by my standards. I should be stronger than I was behaving and I felt a little disappointed with myself. This behaviour was not why I had gone through so much pain, and it was not a behaviour I wanted people to see from me, or an impression I wanted to leave with anyone. It wasn't who I was.

I walked back through to the living room. Jeremy looked up at me, really seeing me being there in his house for the first time since we'd arrived, as if he hadn't noticed my presence before.

'Thank you.' He looked deep into my eyes as he said the words that he truly meant. I didn't need to respond. 'I think I need to be on my own now though, to try and sort it all out in my head.' He continued. I didn't take offence; I could see that he was ready for some space before he even said it. And he could be kind of blunt at times anyway, it was just his way. It was a trait I had always liked about him. At least you knew where you stood with him. There was nothing fake about Jeremy. A few people I knew could learn a lot from him that's for sure.

'I'll call you in a few days, check in, see how you are. Call me if you want to talk before then though. I'm only a phone call away.' I called to him as I was letting myself out the front door.

I stood on his doorstep and took a big deep breath, really taking in the fresh morning air. It made me feel alive, and happy, especially after being stuck inside Jeremy's house for the last few days. Without a working phone to call a taxi, or my car parked nearby, I headed to the nearest bus stop. As I reached the bus stop there was a queue of people who all seemed tense, getting ready to hustle off to their days activities, with whatever that held. I'd never seen so many people waiting for a bus locally. The queue snaked its way along the footpath and looked very uninviting. I changed my mind about the bus. I wasn't ready to join a queue, stand in line, and run the risk of possibly ending up in a meaningless conversation with someone in that said queue. It was four miles to my house from here, and I quite fancied the walk and some time on my own with just my thoughts bouncing around my head. I wanted to take in the beautiful trees that my town boasted about often, to hear the morning birds singing to me, to just be at one with me. Me. That was an interesting thought to ponder upon. The bus pulled up at that point, I could have easily hopped on and made things easy for myself, but I didn't want to. That thought of ME was really tugging away at my mind and I wanted some space on my own to explore that thought. I headed off down the path to the park, that would then wind its way thought the various parks and open spaces, eventually taking me home.

Me. I'd started out as a me that wasn't very happy with the outside shell and associated bits. I'd done something about that, I'd changed that shell to something that represented what I felt on the inside. Now the 'me' I had created was stressing about not being liked as the 'me' that everyone in the outside world saw. But did I even like me? That was the question I was asking myself. And it was a question I gave some real thought too as my feet pounded away on the footpath, rhythmical, carrying me in an automatic fashion along the winding route. It was the kind of deep thought you can't speak out loud about, can't describe to anyone else, the kind of thought that talks loudly around the inside of your head with what feels like a million thoughts that only you can understand, that you can only talk about to with the other you that is inside your head. Snippets of memories from the past pop in and pop back out again just as fast. To try and explain what that memory was or what it meant to anyone else would distract the thought process from taking its natural route, taking your mind away from where it wanted to naturally go, and I wanted my mind to go there, to think, to remember, as fast as it needed too. I wanted to remember who 'me' was, I wanted to remember the things that made me, the inside me really tick. And it was then it struck me. Those things hadn't changed. Why would they. The personality of 'me' on the inside had always been there, I had always been the same. Why wouldn't I be?!

Before I knew it, I had reached my front door, I couldn't remember half the journey or the things my eyes had seen as I had walked, my mind had been so busy sorting through my life's events that it hadn't the capacity to take in my surroundings as well. But I felt invigorated by the walk, and the thinking. I felt so alive and excited about my future, and whatever that might hold. I'd come to the positive conclusion that I actually did quite like 'me', and I had missed 'me', a bit. I think I'd got stuck somewhere along the process, in between all the operations and drugs and counselling and maybe now I had finally caught back up with myself. When I'd analysed it I decided that I did have a good life outlook, I was always kind to people, I liked people, and I liked being with people. Basically I liked to have fun, enjoy life and not hurt anyone along the way, what more could you want from yourself? I'd hidden my inside self when I was unhappy with the outside. I'd been brave and took steps to free the inner me. And then I thought I was being a happy person as I now liked the outside that I saw, but there was a tiny snippet missing in the whole picture and I'd not realised what that was until today. It was the inside 'me'. I think my subconscious had thought that I had to change the inside too, when all the other stuff was changing, just to be me, just to be a woman. But it didn't. It really didn't, as that was me, it was just the outside now matched the inside, and surly that was what I had wanted all along. It was why I had started this long and emotionally and physically painful journey. It was why I had spent a fortune to put things right. It was why I was willing to lose family and friends over it. I was a strong confident female, and if my new boyfriend didn't want me, so be it, I would survive, I had survived far worse, and I would move on. It was a walk I wish I had taken months ago. Four miles can change a lot in a person, for the better.

STEVEN JAMES, 1ST AUGUST 2PM

I sat at my desk staring blankly at my computer screen, the words in front of me blurring into one another forming a grey snake across my view. To an outsider it looked as if I was really concentrating on my work, my focus on the document 100%, do not disturb that man, but that was a far cry from the truth. My face never showed much expression anyway, so this was the look my colleagues generally saw from me on a day-to-day basis. I knew my faults. To them this was just another day with the quiet weird man sat at his desk. But the eyes can hide a lot, if you are clever. Instead of focusing on the job on my computer screen, my mind was mentally typing out an e-mail to her, my lady friend, my girlfriend. I think we had reached 'girlfriend' status, but as I had not heard from her in a few day days I was starting to wonder, and it was starting to upset me. I didn't know what to say, she had said she would invite me over for dinner, so how do you message someone and ask, 'when can I come for that dinner?' I didn't think that was the done thing really. I'd finally finished the big project I was working on at work, so I could tell her about that in my message I guess, and that might prompt the dinner invite I was so desperate for. She may have interpreted my behaviour the other night as someone who didn't want to be disturbed until my project was completed, I'd been accused of that before by people, even though I wouldn't have minded being disturbed by her but how was she to know that. I think I needed to look at the vibes I gave off to people. I could be quick to blame everyone around me for things, but maybe I had to take some responsibility for situations too.

My problem is I don't cope well if things don't happen as they are supposed to, in the correct order that I have set out for them to happen in, in my mind. That stress doubles if firm plans have been made and are not followed through. I don't like plans changing, especially when its last minute. If someone said they are going to invite you to something, I am almost sitting waiting for that invite to arrive. It sort of eats away at me, and I can't stop it. My brain doesn't cope if that invite doesn't come, or whatever it may be that I am waiting for. For example, if someone is meant to be at work, I don't like the last-minute change to them not being there, even if they claim they are sick. It's like I need things to be 'just so', and I take people at their word. It means I get hurt a lot, or sometimes annoyed when plans or a set order changes. It's another one of those personality traits I developed that I put down to my biological parents not being there when I was young. I needed someone to blame. I know I do it, and I know other people don't work like that, I just don't know how to change or stop being like it. I know it wasn't my parents fault they died, but there is part of me that can't compute what happened to them either, and subsequently what happened to my childhood. Parents were meant to be there to raise you, why would they not be there to raise me, why would a parent leave a child alone in this world. Maybe I just mentally blocked stuff out now to protect myself, I don't know. I'd never really spoken to anyone about it, and I'd been too young at the time to understand or question anything that happened to me in the months that followed their death. Most people had put my behaviours down to me grieving and had comforted me with that emotion in mind. My adoptive parents were the only ones who thought outside that box though. They seemed to really get me and what made me tick. They made sure everything was just as it was meant to be, nothing was ever out of order. Life worked well with them and I did love them very much for the love and support they gave me. I've always thought they must just be like me, we must all be the same kind of person in how we think, and how lucky I was they chose to keep me. I wondered now if my real parents would have had the same personality traits, as we were biologically connected. Would life have been 'just so' with them had they survived. Maybe they wouldn't have been the same as me, maybe they wouldn't have understood me and my ways after all, and that's why this happened in the first place. I stopped they train of thought just there, it wasn't going to do me any good, and I never liked to have any negative thoughts about my biological parents when they weren't here to defend themselves.

I occupied my mind and stopped the negative thoughts by composing that e-mail I had started in my head. I began by telling her about all the things that had happened in the last few days with me, and how the project had all gone to plan and how relieved I was about that, and that it had finally come to an end. I was hoping this would be the trigger that would prompt that invite to her house in my direction. I might be feeling annoyed the invite had not yet arrived, when it should have in my mind, but equally, I really wanted to see her as I was missing her easy company and I wanted her to invite me for dinner. The office was its usual sombre self and I was craving a decent conversation with someone about something other than work. I hit send, and then immediately went back to the document I was working on. Working always closed my mind to things in the real world, kept my thoughts at bay, and the work was still important to me, so I didn't mind it now the e-mail was on its way to her. Even though part of me didn't want to be thinking about work, or talking about work, my mind had this ability to concentrate and work hard until I was ready to think about other stuff again. It was like I had my own filing cabinet in my head and I could open and close draws to suit the situation, put things away for later, open another draw and get on with something else. I pushed close the 'love interest' draw, and opened the 'work draw', the draw which would make the afternoon go quickly, and the draw I was being paid to have open at the moment.

I managed to refrain from looking at my personal e-mails again until I got home. I'd not wanted to get distracted, or upset, depending upon replies or non-replies whilst I was still in the office. I was pleased I had waited as there was a response sat in my in-box, but it had only come in half an hour ago whilst I had been driving home. I opened it with anticipation, nervous of the simple click that could change everything in an instant. I scanned through the content of the mail fast, looking for key words hoping they would leap off the screen at me. There was some chit chat content that I was too anxious to take in on my first read through. I could re-read that later dependant on the rest of the e-mail. I let out a breath I hadn't realised I was holding in as I saw it, about half way down the page, the invite I had been waiting for. An invite to her house for dinner, just as she had promised me. It made me very happy and life was once again back in order. I e-mailed straight back accepting the invite, with a thank you of course, but I realised after I sent it that I hadn't re-read the rest of the mail, and therefore hadn't commented on anything else except the invite! I wouldn't have been offended by that if I had received my response, but maybe she would. Actually, who was I fooling, I would have been totally offended by that. I really did need to look at my behaviour. Sadly, I couldn't change my response now, the e-mail had gone and now I could stop thinking about the invite and just look forward. I could re-read the e-mail and talk about the content when I see her, gives us something to start the conversation off with. I was comforted by this thought and it stopped me worrying. All I had to do now was to focus on work for a few days to keep me entertained and have in my mind that I would get to see her in a couple of days' time. Life, as far as I was concerned, was good again.

MIA, 3RD
AUGUST 6PM

I felt rather relaxed for a change, I quite shocked myself considering tonight was the night. My 'time out' had clearly helped. It was a nice feeling and I wanted to try and enjoy and embrace it. I had prepared our dinner during the day, getting the worst of the washing up out the way. Considering the size of my kitchen I didn't want the place looking cluttered, and I no longer had a dishwasher where I could hide dirty utensils away from my guests. The dinner could just be popped into the oven when he got here, and look after itself browning off whilst we talked, meaning I wouldn't be stuck in the kitchen all night on my own and him stuck in the other room on his own. It's always hard if you are only cooking for one other person as they then feel they need to come and stand with you in the kitchen or sit in the other room on their own, not knowing what to do, and my kitchen was only really big enough for one person. A guest milling about in it didn't help. Groups can sometimes be easier to host for as your guests entertain each other, leaving the host to crack on with the cooking. I didn't want that tonight though, I wanted this to be a relaxed evening for just the two of us. I wanted the evening to reflect my new-found mood. It's strange how quickly your mind set can change on things. The simplest thing can happen in your day or week and just turn your mood or thoughts in a totally different direction to where they were heading before. I'd felt so happy and relaxed about life in the last few days, and I wasn't worried about this evening or how it might unfold at all. Of course, I still cared about how it went, I wasn't that laid back about it, but I wasn't stressing and overly worrying about it like I had been of late. I really liked him, and I didn't want to lose him now, and I would still be heartbroken if he walked away at the end of the night never to return, but it's how I would deal with that situation if it occurred that had changed. I would survive, and I would move on, I realise that now. The most important thing that I needed to come out of tonight was that I couldn't keep the lies hidden anymore, no matter what the outcome. Not lies as such, more truths, as technically I hadn't lied, just not told him everything he needed to know about me so he could make his own decision on whether he liked me or not.

The doorbell rang, and my heat jumped up to my throat and skipped a beat. Maybe I was more excited to see him than I had been letting onto myself. The inner you is the one that knows all…. I should listen to the inner me more often I think. And not just regarding my choice in men!

'Good evening!' I greeted him as I opened the door and invited him in. We gave each other a hug, and a peck on the lips. I was pleased to discover his gentle kiss still sent tingly feelings shooting all over my body like popping candy in my mouth. I had toughened up, but not that much. I didn't want to lose that and didn't want to block all emotional feelings again. Those days were over. It was a fine balance getting it right.

I took him through to my living room. I could see him looking round at my small house, taking it all in, absorbing who I really was behind a closed door, but there was nothing judgemental at all in his eyes or facial expression as far as I could tell. He just seemed to be looking. I hoped that was really the case behind his eyes. If only he knew the truth about my finances. Maybe he would understand by the end of the night.

We sat down either end of the sofa, so we could turn and face each other. He had so much to say about the project he had been working on, the project that had cut short our last date, the project that had caused so much upset in my mind. I didn't want to interrupt him though and change the subject, he seemed so passionate talking about it and that was nice to see in someone. It showed he cared about things and that was a nice quality to see. But it was also another nail in my coffin as to how silly, childish and insecure I had behaved that night. This was a man who cared about his work and wanted to do a good job, and I had been far too emotional about it all. I had been really unreasonable that night, and I hoped he hadn't noticed. Back to tonight, and he was still engrossed about the project. I hadn't said much about me yet, but I knew his line of conversation would run its course eventually and we would move onto other topics, or subjects that I wanted and needed to talk about with him. I wanted it all to come out naturally in a conversational type way, the flow of the evening was working okay for me at the moment. I didn't want it to appear like I was making a big announcement, we were still in that 'getting to know each other' stage in reality, so new things about each other's pasts were bound to pop out into conversation here and there....

From the kitchen I could hear the timer ding signalling that our dinner was ready. I had laid my small kitchen table with cutlery, wine glasses and a small candle. It looked lovely, I had to say, considering it was usually pushed into the corner and piled high with mail and ironing. I don't know why I did that, almost annoyed I didn't have my old beautiful table to entertain from, but small can be beautiful too. I'd been in such a panic last time we met, wanting the night to go in a certain direction, getting upset when it didn't that it had sort of ruined the night. I didn't feel like that tonight at all. I just felt happy, and what would be would be. Nothing from tonight would kill me, everything was survivable, especially rejection, if that is what happened in the end. Rejection was better than desperation, I kept reminding myself of this.

I served lasagne with some garlic bread on the side, though I already knew I would leave my bread after picking at it to make it look like I had eaten some. Even with my new-found confidence about things I still needed to be careful about my weight. Not because of anyone else, but because I wanted to, and it made me feel good about my new body. We both took our seats and he poured us both a glass of wine. We lifted our glasses and chinked them, as you do.

'Here's to us.' He said as our glasses met. They made a lovely sound, and so they should the money they had cost me.

'Here's to us.' I replied. Our eyes locked across the table, and we both smiled at each other. I loved the way he looked at me, I don't think things had changed for him at all. It was as he had said, he had been busy at work, he'd had a tight deadline to meet, and sometimes that took priority over social engagements. I got the feeling he was quite 'black & white' about things. What you saw was what you got. There was no hidden agenda or altera motive with him. It made me feel bad as I was a bit more 'grey' with my agenda, things not totally as they seemed. I didn't let the thought run away in my head and ruin the moment; I was enjoying his attention too much.

We made a start on our meals, before it all got cold. I think he was quite hungry as once he started tucking into his food there was no stopping him. He made the polite encouraging sounds that people seem to make during his first few mouthfuls, it made me smile. I decided against saying anything serious just yet as I didn't want him to choke on his food. Instead the conversation was very light hearted, skipping from my work and the comings and goings in the office, to his adoptive parents and upbringing, though that bit of the conversations wasn't so light. He'd had quite a traumatic childhood by all accounts, but he appeared all very chilled about it, and clearly loved his adoptive parents as if they were his own.

I'd cheated with pudding and had brought a shop made cheesecake for us to share. Strange how in days gone by I'd have made everything from scratch for a dinner party, when at the time it was never expected of me, and now people might expect me to make it all myself and I end up taking the short cut option. Stereotypical ideas still existed, but actually I didn't mind. I wanted to cook from scratch, I wanted people to expect that to be my role, I liked how that made me feel needed. But for tonight shop brought was just easier. I blame my kitchen too. Its size didn't inspire me to cook lots of home bake stuff. And there was the time factor, I took a lot longer to get ready these days. That sounded like a lot of excuses, even to me but it was what it was.

The night was running away with us and I still hadn't told him. I probably wasn't helping the situation. It's very easy to not say anything and just get on with enjoying the night, but I would feel angry with myself the second he left if I hadn't said something. I was starting to think I might not get the chance either as after dinner he took hold of my hand and led me over to the sofa, all thoughts of washing up pushed firmly to the backs of both of our minds. He started kissing me, and I didn't stop him. I didn't want to stop him. I couldn't tell him now. I didn't want to tell him now; I didn't want to ruin the moment. My body wanted him more, my mind wanted him, and I didn't want to deny my body or my mind of their desires. I didn't want to stop him, but as our clothes started to make their way to the front room floor in our passion to touch each other's bodies, I knew I needed to make my excuses and pop to the bathroom. I just hoped that action wouldn't be the thing to ruin the moment. We could just make love right here on the living room floor. We could do it anywhere in the house for that matter, there were no rules, it didn't always have to be in a bed. But this would be far easier for us both if I could lead him to the safety of the bedroom where I could slip into the bathroom on my way by. So that is what I did, I took control, and led him up the stairs. I pushed him into my bedroom, as I fell into the bathroom. It would only take me seconds, everything was to hand, he hardly noticed I'd done it, especially as I came out of the bathroom with my panties handing from my finger in a very inviting fashion. He pulled me into him, taking my underwear from me and letting them fall to the ground. His hand slowly moved down my back, his fingers taking in every detail of my body as they passed over my curves. His hand moved around my body, sliding its way down. I let him slide his fingers between my legs. I let out a light groan as my mind exploded. He didn't pass comment to my wetness, if anything it seemed to turn him on more. He pushed me to the bed, his body now above mine, masculine, and powerful. All thoughts of the truth were far from my mind as our bodies began melting into one. It all felt so natural, so right, I couldn't stop the feelings racing through every inch of my being. This was far better than the first time. My body knew what it was doing this time, and it craved the feeling it knew it was going to get.

Afterwards we lay in each other's arms, neither one wanting to move and end it. He was playing with my hair, letting it fall between his fingers, I glanced up at him, his gaze a million miles away in the happy place people go to after sex.

'I guess that makes us pretty serious?' I asked without thinking, looking for a reaction.

'I guess it does.' He looked down at me, the intensity in his eyes just as strong as when he first arrived this evening.

'In that case, there is something I need to tell you. His loving gaze quickly tuned to a look of concern. I could feel he wanted to curl into himself and cover himself up, suddenly unsure of the situation he was in and feeling very exposed as he lay naked on my bed, only he can't move as I am still laying on his arm, and I have no plans to release him whilst I tell him what I need to say.

'I have a son.' There, the truth started spilling out of my mouth. I could see him thinking, I was living in a tiny one-bedroom house, where could I hide a son. He was obviously playing though this in his mind, the things he had seen in my house, none of which would belong to a boy of any age.

'Oh, right. A son. How old is he?' I could see him calculating that I would have had to have been a child at the time to be the mother of a grown-up son.

'Thirteen.' I replied. 'And he doesn't live with me, before you ask. In fact, he no longer talks to me.

'Oh. Does he live with his father then? Or did you adopt him out?' He asked quite directly, options clearly running through his mind as to what could have happened to my child. That thought would not even have crossed my mind but given his upbringing I guess that would be a possibility he would consider, and a cruel one at that as far as he was concerned given the sadness behind his own adoption.

'Life is never as it seems, is it?' I say. 'Everyone has a story to tell, nothing is straight forward, but it doesn't change who we are in the inside though. Please remember that.' I take hold of his hand as I continue. 'I should have told you right from the start, but I hope that you understand it's difficult for me, especially as he won't talk to me anymore, can't talk to me anymore. I carry a lot of hurt and guilt over it all, it's on my mind most of the time. I've always found it hard to trust people, and this doesn't help improve that.' Even to my own ears that sounded as if I was putting the blame on the shoulders of my only child, and that wasn't what I had meant at all, none of this was his fault. He was just a chid caught up in an adult problem.

'He's still your son though, and a child. He has to live

somewhere! You've not answered my question, where does he live?' There was no malice to his voice, just a concern for a little boy he doesn't even know, because he was once that boy without a mum. So I tell him straight. 'My son lives with his mother.' I let the statement hang whilst I still held his hand. His gaze returns to being a million miles away, only this time it's a very confused gaze that's taken control of his eyes. Who wouldn't be confused.

MIA, 4TH AUGUST 8AM

I woke to tousled sheets and an empty bed. It was not what I had wanted really, but it enviable given the conversation we had and was how I had gone to sleep, on my own. So it wasn't an unexpected vacant space that my arm stretched out across towards. I wasn't sure how we had left things last night, after my big announcement, but right now that was at the back of my mind. My emotions sitting on the fence about it all, about everything, except my son. The admission about his existence had slapped me in the face as much as it had to my boyfriend. As the words had left my mouth I was hit with the reality at just how selfish I had been for the last few years. To everyone. I should have fought for him more; he was only a child. My poor little Oliver. I shouldn't have given up so easily on my own flesh and blood. But it had been easier to give up, when I had so many other challenges going off in my mind at the time. Was easier for me than to have yet another battle. At the time I thought I was doing the right thing for him but now I am doubting myself, I think I had done it for me.

My poor boy. What a difficult start to life he had had. I hoped it wouldn't affect his future, but I knew in reality it would have some kind of effect on him, of course it would. We'd never lived together, his mother and I, even before my boy had arrived into this crazy world from the safety of the womb. His mother and I weren't even together anymore as a coupe when he did make his arrival into this world, and I'd not been allowed into the labour ward to share the experience of his arrival. It hadn't been a long-term relationship, none of them were for me in them days, and I'd felt a bit used by her at the time. It was like she'd planned it all along and had just wanted me for my sperm, of all things! She'd clearly just wanted a baby, and I had been the fool to provide her with what she needed to achieve just that. I fitted what she needed from a provider in more ways than just my sperm... she wanted someone who didn't want commitment to her and who had a heathy bank balance to go with it. And I'd been paying for it ever since in more ways than one, and I would be for a long while yet. She might have blocked me out of Oliver's life, but she was still happy to take her monthly payments from me to help raise him. With so much going on, the operation, my mental state, that payment and what it symbolises hadn't crossed my mind, or my mind hadn't let it cross, maybe to protect me, I didn't know anymore. It was just a sum of money that left my bank each month, a bit like a mortgage. Was easier not to think about it. How horrible was I? Had I really gotten that selfish I asked myself yet again?

Tears stung my eyes as I thought about my boy, Oliver. The image of his childlike face had been pushed far away to the back of my mind for a long time. The updates had long stopped coming through to me too, and the yearly school photo that I had always treasured didn't arrive anymore either. I didn't even know how that cute little face of his had changed over the last few years. Had the onset of teenage years started to turn him into a man? I just didn't know. And there were certain genes I hoped he hadn't gotten from me; I did worry about that. Was what had happened to me something that he could have inherited. I hoped he hadn't been born in the wrong body too. I didn't want this life for a child of mind. I didn't think my situation was genetic, but then again, I didn't really know how or why I had been born this way so I wasn't sure, and who would I ask such a question too? It wasn't long after I'd been to see my own mother and had told her about me and what was happening that the updates from my Oliver's mother had stopped arriving. I guess my mother had stuck her ore in there and told my ex my news for me. And she'd have gone about it in a negative way that would ensure I was seen as the one who was in the wrong, because my mum would have gone there looking for sympathy, for her, and how hard this was for her. It was always about her. She could be a little selfish like that my mum. Maybe I had inherited that trait from her.

I was never allowed to make the initial contact with Oliver, or his mother. It was always on my ex's terms and timescales. It was usually only when it was convenient for her, or that's the way it seemed to me anyway. I'd have my son for the odd week here and there if his mum wanted to go away, the odd evening during term time, or the occasional weekend, but always when it suited his mum. Of course, I'd always drop what I was doing to spend time with Oliver, so we'd had a reasonable relationship all considering. That was up to a few years ago though. I tried to call once, when I realised, I'd not heard from her for a while, but the call had left me feeling hurt and angry and given my emotional state at the time I hadn't followed it up again. Shame on me, I thought to myself now. Today that would change.

As I pulled up to Oliver and his mums house and turned the car engine off I had a sick feeling in the pit of my stomach. It was like I had only parked here a few days ago to pick my boy up, yet it was a whole lifetime ago, and a whole other person ago that had been here to collect him. It had been years since either of them had seen me too, especially as the real me, and I realised that neither of them would probably recognise me as I am today. I was suddenly doubting my decision to drive over here. I sat in the car, not knowing what to do. Did she even tell him what had gone on, or did my boy just think I didn't care about him anymore? The thought of that hurt me even more. I'd rather he knew and chose not to talk to me than spend the rest of his days thinking I didn't care or love him. With trepidation I got out the car and walked up to the front door. I knocked and waited. It felt like ages, just standing there with only the sound of my heart beat for company. Maybe they were out and I'd have to force myself to come back another time. Then I heard the key turning in the inside lock. And then she was stood there. My ex, looking lovely, the anger I was used to seeing gone from her face. For a brief moment at least. She starred and starred and then the penny dropped and she realised who I was, and that anger and hate she had for me returned, her eyes darkened and her jaw line went all tight.

'I thought you'd got the hint. we don't need you.'

'You're happy to still take my money though' I couldn't help but bite back.

'Hummh' Was all she could manage.

'Is he here?' I asked.

'No. He's at a mates house. I guess we should talk though.' And with that she opened the door wide to me, inviting me in. Something I had not been allowed to do since she moved to this address 8 years ago.

'Take a seat.' She pointed to the sofa. No cosy cup of coffee was offered to me, not that I would have accepted, I didn't plan on staying too long.

'Look. I know I'm being hard, keeping him from you, but you've got to admit, it's a lot to take in. I mean, I don't get it, what you have done to yourself, how's a kid meant to understand what's going on with you?'

'I know. But I'm still his dad.' The words were out before I could stop myself. My sperm had fathered a child, but could I still be a dad? I didn't know the answer to that question.

'Do you know how hard school is for kids these days?! A dad who looks like a mum, or having two mums when he use to have a dad, what's he meant to tell his friends? And I don't want the other mums thinking I'm lesbian either. It's confusing for me too you know.' She paused for breath but seemed to have a thoughtful look on her face, like there was more to come. This was most she had spoken to me since we were briefly together as a couple, and I didn't want to stop her now.

'I mean, we slept together as man and woman, and now you wear better make up than me! It's confusing.' She paused again. 'Look, I do know I was a cow to you back then, with access and all that, and not letting you be there as much as you wanted to. Even before all of this.' She pointed to the skirt I was wearing. 'I just didn't want you getting ideas of custody and being too involved in his life, like some blokes do. I wanted him all to myself, if I'm honest. I know that's wrong, now. But this, this is something else altogether.' She was pointing at me again.

'And you've got that now, haven't you, what you've always wanted. Him all to yourself. Seems like I did you a favour really' She didn't respond, the truth there for us both to see.

'I didn't choose none of this you know. You told me you was on the pill, why? I didn't choose to father a child, we didn't make plans to be parents together, you took away all of my choices. It wasn't an 'accident', you chose, I didn't. And I didn't choose all of this for myself either.' I was the one now gesturing to my skirt.

'I didn't wake up one day and think *oh I'll have a go at being a woman*. It was there inside of me all along. Life would have been easier if it wasn't, but I couldn't choose that either.' I paused, there was a silence as we both let things sink in. Things we had never spoken about, things we should have spoken about many years ago. And I'd just been more open with this woman that I had hated at points in the past than I had been with people who I really did care about. But then she was the mother of my child, and I strangely enough I felt a little bit sorry for her right now.

'Does he know? About me I mean, about who I really am?' I ask, almost not wanting to hear the answer, whatever she says next guaranteed to hurt me.

'No.' She replies. 'I couldn't do it to him. He idolises you. Who you were.' She corrected herself. 'I think it would be too much for him to take in right now.'

A tear slid down my face, I couldn't hold back. She leans down to a box of tissue she has on the floor and pulls one out and passes it to me. I take it and dab my face trying not to smudge my makeup.

'So does he think I don't care about him then? That's worse, in my eyes. I love that boy!' I can feel my temper starting to rise, my emotions all jostling for place to be at the front.

'No. He knows you cared and that you loved him very much.' She replies.

'Cared? Loved? Past tense.' I question.

Yes. Cared and loved.' She says. 'He thinks you are dead.' Her eyes avoiding mine.

'Holy fuck.' Is all I can say as the reality seeps in. I wasn't expecting that at all. My poor boy has been grieving for his father. Something that will probably scar him for life and change and shape the man he becomes. What have I done to him? Should I have not changed myself, should I have stayed as his father and not chosen the path to my own happiness. Is that what real parents did all the time, in one form or another?

'Why? Why would you say that to him?' I ask, confusion taking hold, I have so many questions I don't know what to ask first.

'It was all I could think to say to him, after your mum came here to see me. I was only trying to do what was right for the boy, you've got to understand that.' She desperately tried to defend her actions.

'You could have spoken to me about it. I am still his father, no matter who I am now.'

'You don't even get that do you! It's why it's taken you so long to turn up here, because you don't get it! How the hell is a young lad meant to make head nor tail of it, of you?'

And she was right. How was someone so young meant to understand the massive change I had made to myself. Did I even want him to know about this?. I no longer looked like the dad in the picture up on the side board. I picked it up and stared at the face in the picture, once so familiar, but now a stranger to me. She saw me looking at it.

'He insists we keep that there. Do you know how hard that is for me, knowing the truth. Can't deny him that picture though can I. I do have some heart you know. I know I've done wrong in the past, but I'm trying to be the best mum I can be to him, now he thinks he only has me, I have to be his everything.'

I put the picture back in its place carefully. I'd not looked at an old picture of myself in a while, it always left me with a weird feeling, a feeling I could never quite put my finger on and I didn't want to end up in that weird place now. I needed to keep strong.

'What about the future though. You can't seriously let him live the rest of his life thinking I died?!'

'But you have, in effect. Or that's how I see it anyway. The man that he would be looking for as that father figure is no longer here on this planet, as a man, as a father figure. Michael died the day you let them take a knife to you.'

I stand to leave, not knowing how to handle the situation anymore and not wanting to cry in front of her.

'I'll be honest Mia.' She stops me from leaving by taking hold of my hand in hers, such a gentle kind gesture, given the horrible thing she has done to my son, and a touch I had long forgotten. 'You do look amazing. It's blowing my mind a little, I can't get my head round it, but you do look stunning. There was always something odd about you, you just didn't seem to fit into yourself. But I get it now. You look good, you look like you're meant to be that way, a woman. In an odd way, I'm happy for you. I really am. I don't think I could tell you was a man once, if I didn't already know that you weren't born as a woman. I don't think I could tell that you were a man before.'

I was literally lost for words. This woman who had been the bane of my life since the minute she stepped into it had just given me the biggest compliment and confidence boost anyone had ever paid me in my entire life. I could have hugged her right there and then. But she'd also told my only son that I was dead. I didn't think I could look her in the eye again and maintain my composure and dignity. I didn't know what to do or think, and I didn't trust my mouth anymore. I let my hand fall from hers and let myself out the house.

STEVEN JAMES, 5TH AUGUST 10AM

I wasn't sure how to take the news that Mia had a son, was the father of a son. It wasn't what I was expecting, especially as we had both previously said we didn't have children. I had never got why people told lies, and more than one had been told to me by her. I didn't really get the full implications of what she was saying to me either. Or maybe I did but I just didn't want to, didn't want my mind to process the thoughts that were chomping at the bit to be let out. I think I knew what it meant, of course I knew what it meant, but I wasn't sure I wanted to believe it. That sort of thing was for some documentary on TV, not for real life, not in my life. My head was in a spin, and I was back to that loneliness and isolation that had plagued my life for so long. I had thought those days were behind me, now that I had met the woman of my dreams. I had foolishly thought that we might even settle down one day and start a family or our own, but if I was right with my thinking that would never happen, that could never physically happen if I was right. I don't know how I had missed it, had missed the signs, or had I just been blinded with a lust for her and caught up in the moment of it all. It was a total head mess, and so far removed from my usual orderly life.

I'd come into work, more for the distraction than anything. My heart wasn't really in it today to be honest. The office had it usual drab feeling to it, only it was more noticeable today. I couldn't really blame anyone here for not striking up conversation with me about anything, let alone this little bombshell. Why would they break that habit now, to them this was just another ordinary day in their ordinary lives. All my old childhood friends were so far away now I couldn't talk to them either. This wasn't something that I wanted to talk about over the phone. How could I? Firstly, I'd not spoken to them in ages, it would be a little rude to call just because I need them now, though I know they would have listen had I called. But I wanted to gauge someone else's reaction to the information as I gave it to them, see if my thinking was correct, and you couldn't do that unless you sat down and told someone the whole story face to face.

Sat in my self-made cocoon at work I tapped away at the keyboard, the click click click of the keys echoing around my head, the rhythm soothing in a funny kind of way. I looked like everyone else in here, keen and working hard, but projects and deadlines were low on my agenda today. I was so absorbed in finding the truth I hardly noticed those sat around me, or where I really was. I typed *man changing into a woman* into goggle and just prayed that the powers that be at Head Office never really checked the browsing history of their staff's computers, like they sometimes suggested they did. Imagine the rumours from that little discovery! And the awkward disciplinary talk I'd have to go through. I didn't care though, this new subject matter in my life was all my mind could think about, finding out more about what I think was going on, something I had no understanding of, but a subject that had landed in my life with a thump. How naïve I was, I didn't even know what to call it!

One search result read:
some men what to become a women due to the fact they feel they

are trapped in the wrong body. Switching the sex from what is their physical appearance to match that of their mental and psychological appearance, there you have a transgendered person.

Further reading hinted at men dressing up in woman's clothing for fun. But I knew this was more than just that. I'd had actually physically has sex with her for starters and being blunt, I'm not the most observant, but I'd have noticed a penis getting in the way when we were getting down to it.

I then read some stories about men tuning into woman due to high levels of the female hormone in their systems. Maybe this could be it, like a condition or something? But her penis wouldn't have disappeared surly? My brain couldn't compute what I was reading. There was a whole world out there that I had never considered, never even knew existed, and it was all a bit too much to take in. I felt like I had been living under a rock in the dark ages somewhere whist the rest of the world moved on to the place I now find myself living in. How could I not have been touched by this before now, and I don't mean literally. People changing who they were born as, totally, from one sex to another. It did actually happen. And I had been touched, no getting away from that fact, and I didn't quite know how that made me feel. Did it repulse me? On paper it sort of did repulse me if I was honest with myself. If I had known beforehand that she was once a he, would I have let her touch me on my penis. I really don't think I would have. The idea is a strange one to contemplate, and I hated myself for feeling this way, for being so stereotypically male, but that's how I felt at the end of the day.

But then again, I thought to myself, on the flip side to the logistically side of changing from a man to a woman, I had fallen for Mia, the woman, and her woman bits. I had fallen before this bombshell, and I was starting to love her. I loved Mia, and I think I still did. So how could Mia repulse me? The woman I had wined and dined, the woman I had shared some very special moments with, the woman I had spent many an hour thinking about, dreaming about the next time we would see each other. She has taken up a lot of my emotional time, and it was something that I couldn't just switch off like that. She was still Mia at the end of the day, wasn't she? I hadn't known whoever she was before, when she was a he, I had never met him and had no knowledge of what he was like. He wasn't part of my life, and I didn't want to let him be a part of it. And Mia was still a person, a human regardless of what had gone on, and she still had feelings of her own, and a mind that excited me. This stuff I was reading on the internet didn't seem to fit with the lovely Mia who I knew. This was something way out of my comfort zone, a situation I knew that I couldn't take my usual black and white approach with, an approach that had seen me though many a difficult situation, but not this time. I left my desk to find a quiet corner at the other end of the office. An empty meeting room provided me with the privacy I needed right now. I put my head in my hands, closing my eyes, resetting my thoughts. I needed to speak to someone, to talk this out loud, my head was not helping me at all and I needed another human more than I had ever done in my life before, and the best person to speak to about it would be Mia herself. She was the only one who could answer my questions, she was the only one who could give me the truth, and not just a gut reaction, or worse, a repulsed reaction. I just hoped she was willing to talk to me, especially after I had just left her hanging when she told me about her son, when I walked out without a word. She must be feeling terrible right now and probably needed someone to talk to too herself. As annoyed as I was that she had kept it from me, I could see that it had probably been a hard conversation for her to broach with me. I wonder now how long she had been trying to tell me. Did she try from day one but got scared off when I said I had no children of my own? Maybe she though I wouldn't entertain someone with baggage. Had I given off that impression? Maybe I needed to take some responsibility for her inability to tell me sooner, but there was still no getting away from the fact that she should have told me before she did.

MICHAEL/MIA, 2ND AUGUST 8AM

T oday was the day. Today it was finally here, the day I had been waiting so long for, and I had woken early with excitement, and a nervousness too. Ironically it was two years ago today that I went to my neighbours' BBQ. Or rather my exneighbours BBQ. That had been another momentous day in this journey of mine. A lot had changed in the last two years though and moving to a new house had been one of them major changes to have taken place. It was nothing to do with the people or the location or anything like that, it was more about reducing my outgoings and reducing my money worries, so I had massively downsized my house, and my bills along with it. I'd left my job in the end, I couldn't face going back to it at that point in time and didn't want to take on new employment until after my final operation as it all seemed too much. I just wanted a break from the stress, and to start afresh once I was all sorted.

So today was 'Operation Day'... Something I had drempt about so much. I can't believe it's finally here, the day when I can have the operation that will change my outside shell to finally match my inside soul once and for all. An operation that would free me of Michael and his manliness. Today I was going to have those horrible man bits that had plagued my life forever removed from my body, to be turned into something far more beautiful, in my eyes. And I was as nervous as hell about it all. Who wouldn't be?! There were so many 'what if's' questions popping up in my head, and that was just about the anaesthetic and going under the knife, let alone the concerns I have over the actual operation going wrong. Once that knife has pierced my skin and the surgeon has started cutting away at me, removing bits that can't just be stitched back on there would be no going back. Not that I wanted them stitched back on, but there was so much that could go wrong with an operation, so much that couldn't then be fixed to man or woman. I could end up in limbo forever, but I had to take that risk. This was major surgery and I was going in for it voluntarily but if I didn't, I was guaranteed limbo forever more, with this operations there was a very strong chance I could change that, and finally be able to get on with my life.

I'm sure some people think I am crazy even attempting this final hurdle with an operation. I mean, looking from the outside I was all woman now so why go under the knife again. My breasts look amazing after the procedure I'd had on them, so realistic, and shapely, I'm over the moon with them, but that had been a small fry of an operation compared to what I was about to tackle. And I had been so lucky with my hair too. I'd not been a man plagued with baldness, I had always had a full head of hair, and for that I was very grateful. I wasn't sure how it would actually grow once it was allowed that freedom but it had grown well, thick, strong and glossy, my hair was doing what it had always been destined to do, be long. I'd wanted instantly longer hair when I made the decision to come out, so I had initial gone down the wig route, but I hadn't had to wear the wig for that long in reality. Not like some of the girls I've met during this journey of mine. Some of them girls are going to be wearing those wigs forever, their old male genes stripping them of the ability to ever grow long hair of their own. Before they go to bed, they would have to remove their wigs, and have that constant remind of who they had once been. I felt really lucky, apart from a decent hairdresser who knocked my hair into shape with her scissors, mine hadn't needed much intervention at all. Those poor ladies bound by their wigs with their daily reminder of their past, I'm hoping one day I can forget it all, and put it all behind me.

Even with all this risk, and worry, I know I can't go back now, I can't live with this black cloud hanging over me anymore. I needed to take this risk, for me, for Mia. I sort of feel excited for the future now, once I can get today out of the way, I think there will be no holding me back anymore.

'Mia' The nurse calls to me as she walks into the waiting room, I'm the only one waiting today it seems.
I stand to follow her. 'Are you all prepared for today?' She askes. A strange question I think, before an operation, but then again given the operation perhaps not.
'I am' I respond. 'I know I will be in pain afterwards' I say 'But I just want this over with now. I am more than ready for this operation.'
'I'll be here afterwards for you and I'll help you to manage that pain.' She says in a kindly voice. I just hope she has the authority to administer the strong stuff to me, from what some of the girls have said it can be horrific.
She smiles at me, and leads me through to a private room, askes me to undress and put the gown she gave me on, and then she would be back shortly to start the preparations.

Sat alone in the small medical room I wish that I had someone with me I knew, someone to talk rubbish chat with me during those last moment before they take you down to surgery, someone to take my mind off things and to just simply hold my hand. I felt quite alone today. Some of the girls had offered, but it wasn't fair to accept that from any of them. Afterall they are all dealing with their own shit, and I didn't want any of them to see me in pain and change their minds about their own operations which were coming up. I would never forgive myself if my pain changed someone else's chance of happiness at the final hurdle. And with no family of mine on talking terms with me, still, that didn't leave many people to ask to come and be with me today.

'You can do this girl!' I said out loud to myself. I closed my eyes and put myself in a happy place whilst I waited for the nurse to come back and take me down to the operating theatre.

MIA, 2ND AUGUST 8PM

I woke to find I was laying on a hard-single bed, totally disorientated and extremely groggy. Then I remembered where I was, I was in hospital, and I must be feeling the side effects from the anaesthetic. It all came rushing back and I quickly left the safe cocoon of unconsciousness. A nurse popped her head round the door to my room to see if I was awake yet and she told me the time whilst she was at it. Not that time really mattered to me right now, but people seem to think you always wanted to know what time it was. Maybe she told me the time to help give me some perception on the day, or so I knew how long the operation had taken I don't know, but I didn't care right now anyway. She also asked me if I would be wanting anything to eat for dinner, which I didn't, couldn't think of anything worse than trying to eat right now. I think she was hinting that the kitchen closes soon, I don't know, and I don't really care, I can't think, about the time, about food, about anything real. I just shook my head slowly indicating 'no' and closed my eyes again, hoping this nightmare would all go away. I just wanted to fall back to sleep, back to that safe place.

When I started finally to come around from the anaesthetic a little bit more I started to become aware of my immediate surroundings. I was in a strange room with lots of beeping going on, fast beeps, slow beeps, I just hope they were good beeps. No one around me seemed to be panicking which I took as a good sign but none the less the beeping was making me feel nervous. I could also sense lots of people had now come into the room, and there was lots going on around me, lots of talking to each other, and no talking to me, which only added to my nerves. I felt flustered and hot, I didn't really know where I was, or who I was in fact. For a moment with my eyes closed I was Michael and I didn't know why I was in a hospital, in a hospital bed with all this commotion going on around me. What had I had done... I just didn't know. A thought crossed my mind that maybe I had had an accident. Maybe I was having a flash back in time, but I really thought that was who I was, and something bad must have happened to me. That was until a nurse had said 'Hello Mia' during one of my attempts to open my eyes. Mia... Mia... It took me a moment to realise she was talking to me! I couldn't speak properly; I just didn't have the energy to form words in my mouth... I tried. Instead, I made eye contact with the nurse and sort of smiled, which I think she took as a sign I was OK, I then drifted back into a sleep again, or something.

When I woke again, I found myself back in the room where I had started the day just twelve short hours ago. Just twelve short hours ago I had that last bit of Michael with me still, the last part of his body that proved he had been here on this planet, that he had existed, that he had been real, and now that part was gone, and so was he. I never expected the wave of emotions to flood over me the way they were right now. I'm sure it's the drugs having an effect, playing with my mind somehow, making me think things I didn't want to think and feel things I didn't want to feel. I was so sure, so 100% sure with everything this morning and I had just wanted it done, wanted my penis gone, but now I feel sort of sad, like a grieving feeling for that person you will never see again. I couldn't explain it, even in my own head, but poor Michael had provided for me his whole life. He had the skills to earn me enough money so I could support myself, working in a male dominated environment where a woman would not have succeeded, as sad as that was. He had done that for me, even though he hated it there he had knuckled down, worked hard and had provided me with a firm financial basis to carry on with the rest of my life. He had provided me with the strength and money to go ahead and put myself through this life changing operation. And now, well, now he was dead and gone forever. And I don't know if I ever thanked him for all he did for me over the years. I'd spent so long hating his shell that in the end that there were times when I had wanted him dead, and now he was, and I feel sad and guilty about that. I know it's going to be a feeling I have to carry with me for a while, that guilt and sadness. No-one had told me I would feel guilty. I wonder if this this normal.

Yet there was the flip side to all the sadness that was trying to swallow me up whole. There was the other side of me that was so happy, and so relieved that it was all finally done. That side of me could cry with happiness, and I realise then that I was crying. I think they were the happy tears coming through, not the sad ones. I want to look at myself in the mirror now and see me for the first time, but I can hardly lift my head off the pillow. That glimpse of me will have to wait for now, what's a few days more when I have been waiting a life time. The nurses have me so padded up and covered in bandages that I don't think I would see much of me anyway right now. There's no physical pain yet, that I can tell, only the mental pain, the two extreme emotions battling for pole position, their need more important that the other....it must be the drugs....

MIA, 3RD AUGUST
4AM

I'm awake, properly wide awake, and I don't want to be...
I'm desperately trying to go back to sleep... trying to force
my body to stay asleep, to get back to that place where I can't
feel the pain anymore. Any pain. I think the drugs are starting
to wear off now, the physical pain has well and truly kicked in,
the emotional pain is taking a second place for now, unable to
compete for once. My hand fumbles at the side of my bed, I'm
looking for the nurse's alarm call button which I was told to
press if I needed anything. I think I find it, smooth and cold
under my fingertips. I press what I hope is the 'call' button as
I try to keep my breathing steady, try to stop the panic attack
from taking hold of me. It feels like ages for someone to answer
my call, maybe that wasn't the right button I pressed? But then
again, I have no real perception of time so I couldn't say for sure
how long I was waiting, it just felt like an age, in my room with
no window on my own. I feel hot yet cold and sweaty, its all
happening under the covers, but that could just be the pain too...
I just don't know anymore... I just can't think straight.

'Are you OK Mia?' A nurse finally appears at the door. I've not
seen this one before, I guess she must be part of the night shift,
or day shift, who knows what time it was.

'I hurt so much' I say. I think I mean everywhere, my mind, my
body, just everywhere, but I don't elaborate and let her believe

it's just the physical pain I'm talking about.

'I'll give you some more pain relief' she says, 'and something to help you get back to sleep as well.'

'Thank you' I manage to say to her, but I'm thinking 'that's perfect, I don't want to be awake right now, I can't deal with any of this anymore. 'Knock me out for a long time whilst you're at it!' Is what I wanted to call out, of course, if I'd have said that she would have probably kept me awake, and sat with me, all sorts of alarm bells would have gone off in her head, but I didn't say that out loud, and she had no alarm bells to worry about meaning now I was drifting off again, to that pain free place that drugs send you.....

MIA, 5TH AUGUST
5PM

I t's been a few days now, and the physical pain is either getting more manageable by the day, or I'm just getting more use to its presence within my body, like it's a permanent part of me now. Whatever it was at least I am starting to think straight again, think like Mia, or Michael, I wasn't sure about that bit to be fair, but I was thinking again. But I do know that I've been stuck in this room for what feels like ages now and its starting to drive me stir crazy, these same four walls, no natural light, no other people except the staff that popped in. I felt trapped and claustrophobic. To be fair I had paid for a private room, but now I found myself wanting to be amongst other people again. I'd requested a move onto a main ward, the nurse said I wouldn't sleep as well, but I didn't care. I'd not had one visitor in this private room of mine except for the nurses and the consultant, and their visits didn't count in my mind. I needed to be back in the real world now, and the closest I could get to that at the moment was to be on a ward with other recovering people and see a bit of something going on around me. If nothing else it would give me something to moan about other than my own pain and my constant desire to remove my bandages and have a good look at myself. I was hoping it would also get me away from the mental confusion I am trying to send packing. I wanted to take my mind off me, whoever I was, and to hear about something else, hear about someone else's problems, anything but these four walls and my own voice inside my head. Apparently, I wouldn't really need to be in hospital for much longer, but even then I was only going home to have to look after myself by myself and be stuck with a different set of four walls surrounding me until I was brave enough to venture out into the actual real world. That hospital ward would do for now, it would have to, I don't think I was ready to leave its safety.

'You've got your wish Mia.' one of the nurses came into my room and started bustling about with my drips and drains. I thought she was being sarcastic about my change from being a man to becoming a woman, and perhaps didn't approve of it. I was so shocked I didn't respond to her statement, but she continued with 'We've had a discharge, so we can move you onto the main ward my love.' I don't know why I thought she was being sarcastic, she was one of the kindlier nurses, and had been nothing but gentle and professional to me throughout my stay so far. I think paranoia was starting to kick in as well something the stronger part of my mind was battling to stop dead in its tracks.
'I know you think I'm mad wanting to move onto the main ward.' I manage to reply. I didn't want her thinking I wasn't grateful for her efforts.
'No, not at all my lovely. Just don't be complaining to me tomorrow when you've had no sleep!' She said with a playfulness in her eyes. I knew she wasn't being serious, but she probably did have a good point. I still didn't care right now, I needed to be surrounded by people.

The porter came into my room next. He was to be my saviour and facilitate my move, pushing me out of this room and into the open. Once all the bits I had connected to me that I would need to take had been piled on top my bed he wheeled me the short journey out onto the main ward. My heart skipped a beat when I realised it was an all-female ward. I hadn't even considered that was what would happen, I was just desperate to be with people, but now I realise that I am a woman in full a tear slides down my face. A happy tear, I think.

MIA, 5TH SEPTEMBER 5PM

T ime is starting to go very slow but then fast, it's all very weird and I'm starting to lose perception on it all. I'd been home for a couple of weeks now and strangely I missed the hospital hustle and bustle though I do prefer my own bed at night. I still have regular hospital appointments that I have to go in for, dressings and cone changes, a side of it I'd not really taken in when I had been to my pre operation meetings. It wasn't just a case of simply making me a vagina and that would be that. My body had to get use t having what is effectively a hole down there, where it was once all flesh of some description. To make the hole a normal size I had a series of these cones that needed to be inserted into me. These had to be periodically changed for the next size up to slowly stretch it all out to the size it needed to be. It was a bit like the people you see with spacers in their ear lobes, slowly making the holes in their lobes bigger and bigger by increasing the size of the spacer until they reach the desired size, only this was far more painful, I imagine, and not a fashion statement.

The medical staff seemed happy though with how it was all progressing which was a relief. The scars were healing well, and the most important thing... my penis had coped well with being turned into a vagina, so they say. There was no other way to describe it, and it had been brutal and there was no getting away from that. I had been turned inside out and it would take some recovering from. If I had known about the pain beforehand I'm not sure I would have gone through with it to be honest. That half world I was living in was far easier to deal with than this Well that's how I feel today anyhow. I have not known pain like this ever in my life, and I hoped this would be the last time I was in this much agony. I'd not once imagined the pain level would be so high. Actually, 'high' was putting it mildly. I have never cried so much with pain in my entire life, especially when the cone things are changed for the next size up. I can only imagine it's what it is like to give birth, but even as a woman now that is something I will never get to experience. Being honest though, how I feel today I don't think I would want to give birth anyway, even if the pain was half what I am feeling down there right now, that's not something you'd want to put yourself through more than once, surly?

It had been a long month but had gone quickly as well. That seemed weird even to me. I'd spent so many days on my own that days felt like years, with far too much time to think things over and over in my head, yet I'd been in and out of hospital so much it had sort of broken the days up a bit for me. In one way I looked forward to those appointments, they were my saviour in some ways. This seemed even weirder to me as they only brought pain, but at least they provided me with some kind of routine, focus and company outside of sitting on my own. The medical appointments were all due to stop soon as my outer body was doing so well in repairing itself. It's just a shame that the inside bits of me weren't doing as well. I no longer needed the medical staff to care for me, other people needed them more, only they didn't know what was going wrong on the inside as they couldn't see those bits, and I'd not told anyone how I was really feeling. That was the nature of their job, repair the outside, sustain life, and move on, or so I thought. Only I think

I do still need them in my life. I need the nurses comforting tones to make me feel better for a moment. I need their touch on my skin, that feel of contact with another human gave me such comfort. I was relying on them so much and I didn't want to let go just yet. I've never met a nurse who doesn't ask how you are or how you are feeling. And they ask with such a genuine tone that you think you must be special to them, that they surely can't speak to everyone in that way. It had made me feel loved, liked and cared for. It had made me feel like I had someone on my side for a moment. That feeling they gave me had helped me get through the long days in-between visits when I was just at home on my own, that knowing that there was someone out there who did care for me. In my confused state of mind I think I had turned them into friends who would one day want to meet up at the pub with me. It hurts when you are wrong. Not the same hurt that the operation had caused, that was a physical pain that couldn't be compared to. No, this was a different pain that no tablet can lessen or take away. It scared me a lot. I should have told them how I was really feeling on the inside.

Today was the day I had been dreading since I had woken up from the operation. Today had been the day I had had to face my fears and go it alone. I had just got back from the hospital and I have been signed off! Or 'discharged' as they put it, slightly more medical in its terminology but just the same thing. I still have appointments that I'll need to go to, but these can now be dealt with by my family doctor, apparently, where I'll get ten minutes of attention at best, as long as they are not running behind schedule when appointments are always hurried along. The hospital staffs highly skilled and in demand services were no longer needed by me. As far as the hospital was concerned, they had done their job, they had turned me into a woman, everything looked as it should and it was all working as it should and I needed to get on with my life without them, on my own, as a woman. Okay, they didn't quite put it like that, they were far more professional and gentle in word than that, but that is how I had interpreted their words in my head. That is what I had heard them say. They were the words I had taken home with me. It felt like I was leaving friends behind as I'd walked out of the door, a group of people who I have fallen out with and they no longer want anything to do with me. It felt like losing my family all over again. I tried to tell myself I was being melodramatic and over the top about it all when I was driving home. I didn't understand my own emotions anymore; I think I needed a good slap. But I just couldn't stop those thoughts taking over my mind. I think I need help, but I've been given the all clear, been told I'm good to go.

I close my front door behind me. The quietness instantly killing me as if a knife had gone through my heart. I could feel tears welling up inside, bubbling and fighting to get out so they could stain my face again, only I didn't want to let them do that to me today. I didn't want to break down and surrender to my own self-pity, I had to try and fight this. What right had I to keep breaking down like this. Everything that was happening had all been my own choice, my decision, my doing. People were recovering from serious illnesses right now that they had no choice in having, but I had, and I had to fight it, this emotion, if only to save myself. If I let it all out now I don't think I could stop myself from crying forever and I couldn't do that to myself anymore. A part of the old me kicked in, told me to knuckle down, grow up and get on with it. This wasn't going to happen tonight. 'Put the TV on, chill, watch something light hearted and switch off from thought.' I heard Michael whisper in my ear. His deep voice echoing in my head, a voice that had long since fell silent and left me, a memory I had tried to make myself forget. Maybe that was where I had gone wrong. And he was the only one here for me now, the one who knew me best, inside and out. Maybe he could support me through these dark days. Taking his advice, I did as he suggested and turned the TV on. I stared at it blankly, the quizmaster's voice on some show slowly filtering into my brain, slowly grabbing my attention as I started to think of answers to his questions. My breathing started to slow down, and my tears stared to retract. My mind stopped thinking of all the stuff I didn't want to think about and face. 'Thank you, Michael.' I said to my old self. 'I'm sorry I did this to you.'

MIA, 10TH OCTOBER 8PM

The days were still rolling into one, I had lost all perception of time, and not in a good way like when you are on holiday having so much fun, because I'm not having fun at all. The days are becoming one long bore, with only myself for company and the Michael side of me if he decides to pop in and chat. I've become somewhat of a hermit to real people which was a worry, I felt cut off from the world, and it's a cycle I don't know how to break free from. It's also a cycle that sadly I'm not actually ready to break free from either, the loneliness offering a comfort all of its own. This change of mine, from being a man to becoming a woman, I never envisaged it would bring this level of confusion to my life. I guess I expected that my family would love me unconditionally and would still all be by my side helping me thought the process, but I'd got that so wrong. I think part of me was trying to heal from the rejection by them on top of everything else. And I use to have so many friends around me too, and now I have none. I was starting to think that this was a little bit my own fault though with regards to old friends. Yes, there were people, mainly my family, who had cut me right out of their lives, but there were other people, for example my old neighbours, who had really tried to embrace my change, and understand what I was doing, and at least accepted who I was. And what did I do.... I went and moved away, ran away from everyone who knew me as Michael for that fear they would reject Mia, it was better to put up massive barriers in my mind and protect myself from people rather than be let down again and again by those around me. But was it better I had to ask myself? No one had been to see me since my operation, but then why would they, I hadn't told anyone from my old life when I was going into hospital. As far as they were all aware, I was still a man dressing up as a woman, so why would they come. I think I expect too much from people, I think I want people to make the effort to contact me, to be asking me how it was doing, when was my operation and all of that, but the reality was that actually that is a big ask of people, especially when those people lead busy lives of their own with their own worries and stresses. People who I have cut out are not going to keep chasing me for details, even if they did still like me. Why would they, the barriers were up!

I needed to take back control of my life. I'd woken in a rare productive mood. Only I could sort this out for me, and it wouldn't happen by just sitting back on my butt waiting for life to begin again just like that. I had to grab the world with both hands, and make it happen for myself, before I disappeared too much and would be unable to return. I had made this decision to change from man to woman, to let the real me out into the world, and now I needed to embrace that and let 'me' enjoy the life I could never have before. If I couldn't do that for myself, how was anyone else meant to help me? The question of where I would start had been going around my head for days, and today I came up with an answer for myself. I decided on the shops, an easy place to go on your own, people did it all the time. I needed to go out and buy food for myself and not just order it in on-line as I had been doing, and it was time I treated myself to some new clothes too, to celebrate the completion of my change. That might just help me to feel good about myself and my new body. I'd always loved shopping and had often brought my mum new clothes just for the love of it, things I would really want to wear myself but couldn't at the time, things that I would enjoy seeing her wear for me. Hey, guess what... I could now go out and buy myself anything I wanted to wear and wear it myself, fully, properly, as a full woman. No manly lumps to hide, I could finally wear anything I wanted. I also needed to start exercising again as well.... I'd put on a bit of weight since the operation purely though moping about and binge eating. No amount of hormone replacement and operating on could take away what the male hormone had given to me in my teenage years, a bigger bulkier body. I had changed shape, there was no doubt about that, but I wanted to be all womanly, and not have the remains of my beer belly to show, I needed to lose a few pounds to help enhance my new feminine shapes. The ideas were all starting to bounce around my head now, jostling for position, I wanted to cram so much in, I felt excited, invigorated and I just wanted to get going on it all. I felt alive again.

Today I had a plan. Today was going to be a good day. Today was going to the start of a new me, a positive me. I really feel that today is the day it all starts again, life starts again. I got dressed and left the house without first checking that no one else was around outside. I just opened my door and stepped right out there into the street. It didn't faze me one bit that one of the neighbours was outside trying to get her crying child into its car seat.
'Morning.' I called to her above the child's screams.
'Morning.' My neighbour called back. 'You don't want to swap for the day, do you?' She joked back. Yesterday that would have had me in tears. Today I took the comment how it was meant.... My neighbour saw me as this young free female who is not commencing battle with a naughty child. She saw me as 100% female and was most likely remembering her carefree childfree

days through a rose tinted glass. I laughed at her comment and wished her a good day.

MIA, 9TH NOVEMBER 8AM

My new-found positive attitude was certainly helping my mental state of mind and general wellbeing. Though I still hadn't contacted or actually met up with any friends of mine or anything like that, but still, I felt better about stuff. On the positive side I had found a forum on line, a chat group, for people like me who had made that change and were struggling with it, or just wanted to talk to other people in the same boat. We were a group of unique people in our own right really, only other people who had gone through the operational change would have any real understanding of what we had all done and the challenges we face on a day-to-day basis. Some of the people on the forum got me down a little bit, they were so negative and I just didn't need that in my life, but maybe they needed me. The more I'd get chatting to them the more I realised that actually they were just negative about everything in life, and their 'change' had nothing to do with their attitude, it just fuelled them and gave them something else for them to moan about. There were a couple in particular that I'd try to stay off the forum if I saw them 'active' and online. I don't mind helping but that doesn't do me any good, as selfish as that may sound, I was on there to help myself be normal again, not to be a shoulder to people who never give anything back. On the flip side I have also got chatting to some great people, who have given me some positive tips and advice, and just general conversation about the world we lived in. It's quite a unique thing really, when I think about it. I'm a woman, I always have been, but I couldn't chat t to other woman about certain things as they wouldn't understand what I was going on about. They were born in the right body to start with and had gone through all the normal womanly things that they chat to each other about. My journey to womanhood wasn't like there's at all, I'd followed a very different route. I'd never have a period in my life, or give birth to a child, or go through the menopause in the same way a born woman would do. And it wasn't like I could talk to my old male friends about it either, having once been a man. Some of them are real men's men and just wouldn't understand what I had done to myself. They love their cocks more than life itself, their cocks almost ruling them. To them, the thought about cutting it off and turning it inside out was outrageous. Some of them would rather just die I think, so to expect them to understand what was going on inside of me just wasn't going to happen in this lifetime. I didn't think any less of them for it though, it's just the way the world is, but everyone needs someone who is the same as them to talk about stuff too, to share stories, compare notes and such. Women need other women. Men need other men. And I need other transgenders in my life more than I ever realised I would. It's just not always so easy to find people like me in normal circumstance. Relying on bumping into someone new in the pub and striking up a friendship because we were both trans wasn't that likely. I had to be a bit more targeted in my search for a friend. And that is what I had gone and done. And it had been my saving grace and had put me back on track with life. I was happy to admit now; it had stopped me from falling into some kind of depression. It's just a shame I can't meet up face to face with some of the people I had gotten talking to. Face to face would be amazing, we could have a real chat, real voices, natural conversational flow in a real setting. But we are all spread so far and wide across this world of ours, and I've found the people I've got on the best with, or have chatted the most easily with, are generally from America or Canada. Not an easy pop to the pub and have a meet up and chat on a Tuesday night that's for sure. Or maybe that was an invisible barrier I had put up for myself again, maybe I wasn't ready for face to face, maybe online gave me a safety blanket I wasn't quite ready to let go of. Who knows. Who cares. I was just happy to be in a better place mentally than this time last month, if there were barriers so be it. I felt in time I'd be able to knock them down now, when I was ready.

My exercise and body shaping goals were going well too. I found the running was helping me immensely, and not just with changing my body shape. I always felt mentally good after a run. My body almost felt like it had had an orgasm, and that was something it wasn't getting at the moment, so the running was becoming a little addictive in many ways. My body was starting to look good as a result, my mind was starting to shape up, things were looking up, it was a win win all round as far as I was concerned. I just needed to fill my life with some real people now. People who knew me by name, people who would ask how I was, and who I could return the question too. I needed people who would care about me, and I wanted people in my life who I could care about too.

MIA, 12TH DECEMBER 5PM

I'd been out shopping again today, forgetting the season, I had joined what felt like thousands of people doing their Christmas shop, trying to get all of the gifts they needed in one hit, and in the process their shopping bags got wider and wider and their minds narrower and narrower. I had seen several parents snapping at their kids and had been bashed into with wide shopping bags more times than I care to remember. Mayhem was the only way I could describe it. It sort of made me glad I wasn't joining in with the madness of Christmas this year, but it also sort of made me sad that I wasn't joining in too. I had no one to buy for this year, so my shopping list had only been for me. I couldn't even go and buy my son a gift. I'd not seen him in months now. I'd always liked buying his Christmas presents, it had always made me feel important, and like I had a son, even if I wasn't in his life every day. Instead, this year I'd just put some extra money in his mum's bank account in the hope that she would buy him a really good gift, in her name. That's the way she wanted it, that's the way it was. She'd get all the glory and thanks, but at least my son wouldn't miss out on things in his life. The things we do....

I unloaded my shopping onto my bed. All nice new clothes. I was getting to be a bit of a shopaholic in all honesty. I'd lost some more weight, and my other clothes were hanging off me a bit, and I loved buying myself new clothes so why not. I wanted clothes that made me look good, as I would then feel good. I wanted to stay in this positive up cycle I found myself in, even if it was costing me a small fortune along the way. I was trying not to think about that financial dilemma at the moment. At the back of my mind I knew the bubble would burst at some point, I'd not worked in years now, but that was very much at the back of mine, an issue I would tackle in time, soon. Living in the moment, the sales ladies in the shops, all keen, all helping me, all treating me as the woman I was, making me feel like they were my friend as they complemented the outfit I had tried on. I felt on top of the world with it all, it was making me feel good, it's what I needed right now. I'd worry about the rest another time.

It was still early, and I was guessing a lot of my on-line mates would still be at work, but I thought I'd log on anyway and see if anyone was about so I could show my new clothes off, so to speak. It was too early to call it a night, I was on a high and I wanted to talk to someone. I was in luck, my computer beeped at me to let me know that someone in my 'friends' list was on-line who would like to chat. I opened the icon up to start a conversation and was excited to see it was one of my friends from Canada who was clearly having a boring day at work. We chatted for a bit about her boss, who kept coming onto her. She was hot, if I did say so myself, and unless you knew, you'd never be able to tell she was once a man. Well from her pictures that was the impression I got, and from what she was telling me about her boss I'm guess she was just as hot in person. All joking aside she was in a difficult situation and just didn't know what to do about it. She didn't want to tell her boss she use to be a man just to stop the attention, as she was trying to get on with life as a woman and didn't want to keep referencing back to a person she was no more. Plus, it shouldn't matter that she was once a man, she didn't like him like that and he should just respect that.

I totally got that, but she also didn't want to tell her boss she was in fact gay. She still loved women as she always had. She thought if he knew she was gay that he would make her life difficult at work. He was that kind of bloke, and she'd seen it before with him with other staff members. But what could she do? I suggested the only thing she could do was to look for another job and get herself out of there. It wasn't like she really loved the job or anything, it was just a job to her at the end of the day, something that paid her bills and kept a roof over her head. Made me realise how simple my life was, how easy my dilemmas really were to deal with. I downloaded some selfies I took of myself in my new clothes and uploaded them to our private chat area. It took her mind off her shit, and the positive comments she gave me took my mind off my shit. It was a long-distance friendship that was not really going anywhere beyond what it was, but what it was worked perfect for the two of us so what did that matter anyway. About an hour later we said out goodbyes and I logged off of the forum. I was ready to relax now with a glass of wine and my feet up on the sofa. I needed to unwind, and start planning my next move in life.

MIA, 25TH DECEMBER 9AM

I wake up, alone, and with a long lonely day stretching out in front of me. It would be just like all the other days, but today was Christmas Day and it somehow seems worse than the other days spent alone. Today I have no distractions available to me except the TV, today I can't go shopping to find some companionship and take my mind off things, today I wake up really missing my family. Today I must face me and only me. I'd love to be sat around my mother's large dining table, me and my brothers taking the micky out of her for something or another whist she'd rush about to feed us all. Then after dinner we'd all retire to the living room where we'd share gifts and have a giggle about things that have gone on in previous family gatherings. There would be such a buzz about her house today, there always was at Christmas, only I wasn't going to be a part of it today. My mother always loved hosting Christmas, especially when my brothers went and got girlfriends and especially when the girlfriends then turned into wives. They would come and stay with us as well; it was always such good fun. A large happy family. I imagine my mother now, she'll be up and dressed already, in the kitchen preparing the turkey, flapping about with pots and pans. My father will still be in bed most likely, staying out of her way until she summoned him into the kitchen arrangements when she is ready for him. Everything very much all on her terms on a day like today, but it made her happy, and none of us begrudged her that. Only I wasn't part of that 'us' anymore in their eyes, or mine. My family were still not speaking to me, they didn't even know I was fully Trans'd now, didn't know I was a woman, and I doubt they would even recognise me in the street if they passed me by. I should tell them really, it might be the commitment to the cause that will bring us all back together again, but I wasn't ready for the rejection if that is what happened, and I suspected it would be. I'd not healed from the first rejection yet. Maybe I will write to them in the new year, let them know the updates on me, give them my new address, see if they do come back to me. At least that way the rejection isn't face to face, I might be able to handle that a bit better I think to myself.

I was also missing my own son today, missing seeing his face opening his presents. I hope he wasn't feeling too sad that I wasn't there with him I didn't want it to be a day of reflection for him, grieving a dad no longer there. In some ways that grief would be justified now, his dad as he knew him was dead, but in a way that could mess with his head. I wouldn't want that for my boy. Life was tough enough without that.

I'm all recovered now, well physically I am. All my external scars are looking good, and I don't have a penis anymore, which strangely took a little getting used to, more than I thought it would anyway. I'd wanted it gone from my body for so long, had hated it just hanging there all the time, and then when it was finally gone, I felt a bit guilty like I had killed part of me off without a second thought. But there had been second thoughts, and third and fourths. Strangely peeing wasn't so convenient now either, something I'd never even thought about being an issue before my operation. That moment when you get caught short, a bush is no longer an option for me! It might be for some women, but that didn't work for me, but that was a small price to pay for the massive gain I now have, I think. My vagina. I slowly getting use to her, she's a bit hidden but I've had a couple of exploring moments with her, not as many as I should have had, but none the less I knew it all worked down there. It was still all taking a little getting use too, finally having one of my own to play with, but I also keep feeling like I should let her settle in a little, let her get used to being part of me, it was as if she had only just been born and was new to this world, and in a way she was. I almost feel a bit scared of her, in an odd way.

Mentally, I'm still a bit up and down, good days, bad days, the good days slightly outweighing the bad days now. I have locked myself away in this house since I got back from the hospital, and only venture out to the shops or to go running, noting really social, nothing with real people who knew me. Not having regular contact with real people isn't helping me, it's starting to take its toll on my mind and my mental stability, that much I can see for myself. Part of me feels like people will judge me and think I have done the wrong thing, changing who I am. Some days I lay here wondering if those doubters are right, have I done the wrong thing in going the full hog with the operation. The question I ask myself often is 'was I really that unhappy in the first place, could I not have lived my life out as a man', and in the process kept the people around me who loved me as Michael. I'd have kept my family and kept my son, to a degree. He wasn't a bad bloke, Michael, should I have tried harder to have gotten on with him, rather than killing him off like some character in a novel, easily wiped away, leaving everyone to live happily ever after. Only at the moment I wasn't doing that was I. And it was a question I hadn't been able to answer consistently. Some days I missed him and the life that came with him, other days I feel a little bit more positive about things and love my new body and finally feeling like me. I'm waiting for the time when those positive days outweigh the missing Michael days and I'm starting to get there with that. I didn't even know if that was a normal way to think or feel, and I had no one to compare notes with right now, except my on-line forum, but I was on that less these days too, there is only so much you can go over things with someone you don't actually know, and can't actually see.

I'd cancelled my follow up appointment at the Stony practice with Jeremy, had called and said I was all fine and happy, but the truth was that I wasn't, but I didn't want to verbalise my thoughts out loud with him or to anyone, in case that made my fears true, and it was all too late for that now anyway so why would I put myself though that stress. That was the justification I had used to myself. I didn't want Jeremy to think he had done the wrong thing letting me go ahead with the full change, didn't want him to think he had talked me into it, I had too much respect for him professionally, he didn't need to be burdened with this phase of mine, I liked him too much for that. And I was sure it was just a phase; I'm just hoping I ride it out soon.

Another big worry I have to face soon is my financial funds are finally starting to run low. It's no surprise really what with the way I have been spending m money on clothes. In the new year I need to force myself back out to the world of work, back into the real world, before it's too late and I can't even afford to pay my bills. I'm not sure what work I want to do though, I can't just go back into my old line of work. Well, I guess I could do really, but I just don't want to if I'm honest, not even just to bring in some pennies. I don't want to face all my old contacts. It's that kind of industry even if I went to a different company I'd still see the people I knew from before, and I wanted a fresh start on the work colleague front. I don't want the people I work with day in day out knowing I use to be a man. That didn't need to come into it. I don't know why I feel like that as I shouldn't feel embarrassed about it, but that is how I feel so I have to ride with it. I think I don't want the constant questions I know it would bring with it. I want to be able to walk in to somewhere each day and for the people I work with just to accept me as who I am, no questions, no judgments, we just crack on with the day and maybe talk about that we're all up to at the weekend, I just don't want deep stuff with my co-workers. I'd worry about that in the New Year though, today I just needed to worry about getting through the lonely day and my Christmas meal for one.

I wasn't ready to get up out of bed just yet, not much point really, but someone was banging on my front door, and quite instantly too.

'Okay okay' I call down the stairs as I head to the door whilst trying to tie the rope on my dressing gown together to save at least some embarrassment when I open the door. I was a little worried as to who it could be this early on Christmas day. It wouldn't be my family that's for sure as they don't know where I live now, and at the moment my social circle was non-existent so I never got people I knew visiting regularly, let alone unexpectedly. It must be one of the neighbours I think to myself, and I guess there must be a problem of some sort by the urgency of their banging.

'Hi' I say as I'm opening the door. 'Oh...Jeremy!' I'm shocked to see my therapist stood on my door step on Christmas day. 'Are you OK?' I can't think what he would be here for, today.

'Hi Mia. I'm sorry for the unannounced house call. I just wondered what you're up to today?'

What an odd question I thought to myself.

'I was just going to chill in front of the TV most of the day, watch crap programmes and eat lots. Why's that?'

'Are you on your own?' There was a strange hope in his voice that I couldn't put my finger on.

'Yes I am, thought I'd have a quiet one, what with the year I have had and all.'

'I thought you might be. Would you like to come to mine for the day, have dinner with me and my wife? You're not putting us out, before you ask.'

'But isn't that a bit unprofessional, crossing boundaries and such?' I ask, unsure where all this is all leading too, and why the invite arrived on the day, last minute.com, without time for me to prepare and at least by gifts for them.

'I think you signed yourself off, professional, we've not seen you at the surgery since your operation. And I've always liked you...not like that you understand! But we've always gotten on, haven't we? ' He didn't wait for my reply. 'And I had a suspicion you'd be on your own today and I'd quite like to be friends with you, outside of the surgery. If you would like that, that is?'

Jeremy let the words hang there. Doubt was written across his face, I could see he was questioning himself, had he read something wrong between us, should he have come here at all, on Christmas Day of all days. He was desperate for me to respond and my stunned silence was killing him. I don't know quite how it made me feel, this whole out of the blue knock on the door and an actual 'friends request' in person. It all struck me as a little odd, but whatever was going off in my head right now it was all positive feelings. I'd had a whole host of friends request on Facebook recently, mainly from other trans people who I had only met once or twice, usually at hospital or other appointments, or from the on the on-line forum girls who I'd never actually met. But where were they all now? Not here that's for sure, just a name and a smiling face on a screen. They don't really help you through the dark days just like I don't really help them through theirs.

'I'd love to Jeremy, thank you, if you're sure.' I answered without giving it much further thought at all. That's what Michael would have done, grabbed the moment offered to him by the hands, and enjoy the experience for what it was. This could be just what I needed, and I felt excited about the day that now lay ahead of me.

He smiled, like he'd just opened an amazing Christmas gift. 'That's great! Thank you Mia.'

I'm not sure what he was thanking me for, I should be thanking him, my day had just gone from potentially dire, to busy with lots of unknowns. Just what I needed, and perhaps just what the doctor had ordered for me.

MIA, 30TH MARCH
1:30AM

It was mid-morning and I was sat at my desk at my new job looking around at the hustle and bustle of an everyday office life taking place around me. That's what it was... everyday ordinary. Nothing amazing, noting life changing, nothing out of the ordinary for anyone there... only it had been just that for me... life changing and out of the ordinary. The job was only a bit of admin work for an electronic supplies company, but so far I really loved it and I was enjoying coming in each day. Always a good sign in my mind. It didn't really matter what it was doing, but it was being accepted for a job that mattered most to me, more than most people could imagine in fact. I'd been here six weeks now, and it was all good. It was getting my brain working again and it was making me feel needed by society once more. Everybody needed to feel needed by someone I'd decided. The other girls in the office seemed nice enough, though already in a tightly knitted circle, I could tell it would take a while for me to be part of them or one of them, but they weren't horrible to me or anything, they just left me out of the social stuff a bit, but I couldn't blame them for that. I'd been so lucky to get the job too, writing a CV when you've changed sex can be a little bit interesting, especially when I was applying for a much lower skilled and paid job that I had previously been doing. I played down my past, gave just enough information to get the job, but not enough to scare them into thinking I wouldn't stay long. I didn't know what the right thing to was, did you state you was trans when you applied to jobs? Did it really matter? It shouldn't in my mind, and so I'd opted not to mention it. I wanted Mia to get the job all on her own, and here I was. This year was looking set to be a better year already for me already. Or less stressful at least.

I'd taken another great leap with my road to recovery too. On the strike of midnight on New Year's Eve I'd made myself a resolution that I would get my life back on track and start enjoying being Mia. The job had been number one on the list, to get me out and about for starters, and would help get my finances a little more stable too after all the spending I had been doing, and that had needed to be a priority. I thought it would help with feeling normal again too, and it had done just that. The next thing on the list was to get myself out there... socially that was. In an attempt to do that I'd gone and done something I never thought I would ever do... I joined a dating website! It was both scary and exciting at the same time but it gave me a safe way to meet new people who there was all the potential I could really end up meeting face to face. I love it, and at every possible moment I log on to my account and see if anyone new has messaged me... like I am doing right now. There was a little '1' flashing in red in the corner of my screen letting me know that I had one new message in my in-box. I hoped it was the man I'd been chatting too for a couple of weeks now, I quite liked the look of him, and we were having some fun conversations. I clicked on the in-box to have a look.

'Ahhhh.. never mind' I said under my breath to myself and promptly closed the screen down. It wasn't the one I had wanted to message me, but another man that I wasn't so keen on who kept in semi-regular contact with me. I would open it later and compose a polite reply, I didn't want to look too keen to him, but

I didn't want to be rude and ignore him either. I suspected he had several woman on the go on-line in the hope one would take the bait and meet up with him. Sensible I guess, who wants to stay lonely forever, and that's why we were all registered on site in the first place, to find that one. Sadly for him he just didn't do it for me. All in all, I was loving it though, it was so much fun, being able to safely flirt with men, say what I wanted to say, and take my time to compose my replies, trying my best to make them a little bit funny and interesting. I could take my time to be Mia in the real world, and learn about who I was when it came to chatting to men. Afterall, I was still getting to know me myself, and this was kind of helping me get there. I'd not mentioned on my profile that I was Trans, I don't think it matters, a bit like with the job, and I'm trying to forget about that label as I think the label is what I was struggling with when I first changed. I just wanted to be me, and I don't want 'it' to have a name and I didn't want people to be put off by it. It took me ages to pick a profile picture too. I'd had to practice the art of the 'selfie' to try and get my best, and most feminine angle. I didn't do the pout many woman seemed to do, that really wasn't me, instead I'd tried to look normal, nice and fun. I'd got there in the end, sort of I think. I was happy with the results anyway and that's all that matters, and although I'm not inundated with offers, I am getting messages, which means men are actually interested in me, in Mia! It's boosted my confidence no end, I'm on a permanent high at the moment,

It had felt like a long day at work today for some reason, the first time that had happened since starting here, but finally the end of the working day arrives, and as I'm gathering up my thing to leave one of the girls come over.
'Hey... How you are settling in Mia?'
'Hey.' I reply. 'Great thanks. I'm starting to get there with it all I think.'

182

'That's good.' She replies back with a friendly smile. 'It can take a while, can't it, getting use to a new job, and new people. We're all going to lunch tomorrow, as it's the end of the week, you're welcome to join us if you'd like?'

'Thank you!' I come back, somewhat surprised. It wasn't what I was expecting, or what I was even ready for, but I recognised the olive branch being handed to me as the new girl. 'I'd love that.' I smiled.

'Great. See you tomorrow then.' And with that the brief encounter was over, and I left the office to go home. Little steps, little things. Life was slowly starting to change. I left the office for the day smiling, feeling happy, feeling accepted in the new world I had created around myself.

Thirty minutes later and I'm home, door closed to the world, and my comfy clothes are on. Although we were having a nice March by all accounts, the evenings were still a bit nippy and I had no plans to go out again today. The encounter in the office had left me feeling relaxed and happy, so I poured myself a glass of wine to celebrate this big step towards acceptance. I took my glass of wine over to my computer desk and sat down making myself comfortable before logging onto my dating site. I'd entertain myself for a few hours by chatting to new people, hopefully. I also had that reply to write to that guy I didn't want to see, but I didn't want to hurt his feelings either, I know I'm not the only one who's on the site who must be feeling sensitive, for whatever reason that may be. And it was chatting with someone at least, he was okay to chat to from afar. But what I really wanted to see was if the guy that I did like was on-line too. And that was the real reason I wanted to be on-line!

I wasn't disappointed, he'd replied, the man that I have been chatting on line with for several weeks now, the man that I was most keen on, the man that had been making me feel a whole lot better about life, and a lot more normal about myself. Or rather the profile of the man I was most keen on had replied, and that profile had made me feel all of those things, as I'd not yet met him in person, but that was all about to change. He'd taken the leap and suggested we go ahead and meet in person, on a date, and I wasn't entirely sure how I was feeling about that giant step. I say he'd taken the leap, but that might have been an easy thing for him to ask me out, and for all I knew he may have taken that leap many times before with other women so it wasn't a leap at all for him, just a normal thing to ask and do. I don't know though. I get the feeling that he isn't a 'player', not like most of the men I know, my old self included in that statement. Though I'd had my reasons at the time for being so easy come easy go about women, I wasn't really in to them, and it's a guilt to those women I will have to carry with me for the rest of my life, but for now that is tucked away in the back of my mind, I don't want that emotion taking hold at the moment. I get the feeling that this man I have fallen for online is a true gentle man, kindly, maybe a bit of a loaner himself, which I why I think it might have been a brave leap for him. Or is that just what he wanted me to believe. I'd lived a lie for so long I sometimes forget not everyone lies about their feelings, but still, you never know. Anyway, he had invited me out, and it made me feel good about myself tonight, and that is what I am focusing on and enjoying the feeling of. I wouldn't have been that brave, to ask a man out, especially not this one as I really liked him. This was all so new to me, and in more ways than one, but I couldn't tell him that.... Yet. There I go again with the lies, but I didn't want to think about that, and I didn't know how to stop either. 'Excitement' I said out loud, that's what I was feeling right now, a large amount of excitement, like dancing butterflies in my belly, like electricity racing through my veins. I had been accepted as Mia by a man and I wanted to enjoy the moment and worry about the rest another day. Nothing else mattered to me at this precise moment in time, absolutely nothing at all.

I'd gauged the timing on my reply to him, not wanting to look desperate, and not wanting to keep him hanging too long either. Not in a game playing way, I just didn't want to mess it up by being too keen. I thought an hour was about the right amount of time to leave it, and I guess he felt the same for his return reply to me came two hours after opening that first message from him. I now had a confirmed date, an actual going out in to the big wide world date... whoop whoop!! I felt on top of the world and like I'd won the lottery, it made me realise how lonely I had been as I had never felt this excited about a date in my life before now, or could it be because I had never been on a date with someone of the opposite sex that I wanted to date before, the correct opposite sex that was. I had a million demons in my head battling for attention, wanting to know the answer to questions they had but I was refusing to let them in to my mind, refusing to grant them any space to take hold, refusing to admit they existed. I didn't want to ruin a moments happiness in what had been a difficult couple of years, and a difficult lifetime. I didn't want to know the answers to any negative questions today, or perhaps any day, I couldn't think that far ahead. Today could be the start of a new life for me, today could be the day I say goodbye to the loneliness that had plagued me for so long.

The date for meeting up had been set, it was in a few days' time, and I had a lot to do before then to make sure I was ready, physically that was. Mentally I was ready, I think. I felt like I finally had a purpose in life again, it had been a while, a long while, if ever at all, I didn't really know anymore. That might sound strange to some people, that another person can give me purpose. Some people may think that purpose should come from within, but I couldn't help how I was feeling, and that was just how I felt right now and I didn't really care what other people thought about it either, I couldn't. All I could think about was now I had pressing things I needed to sort out. Firstly, I needed to get booked in and get my nails done with my nail lady, so that they looked their best on the date. This was unbelievably important to me, I was so conscious that my hands were once a man's hands, they had biologically grown that way even if my soul hadn't. I couldn't change that fact, but I wanted them to look as feminine as they could. A manicure and a new set of gels would soon help with that little issue. I also wanted to get my hair done professionally too, on date day, just so I looked at my best. I didn't want the stress of trying to style my hair on the day of my first date. I just hoped the hairdressers could fit me in this late notice, or it would end up taking me ages to get ready. Deep down I wanted to go shopping too, and buy a new outfit for the occasion, but in all honesty I had so many new clothes that I hadn't yet had the chance to wear out of the house that I reined myself in on that one, money was getting a little bit tight and my pay wasn't what it once was, and the hair and nails would set me back a bit money wise as it was.

'Which outfit to wear?' I asked myself as a form of distraction from the thought of shopping. This could be fun. I took myself off upstirs to my crammed wardrobe in my compact but cosy bedroom and started pulling outfits out ready to try on. I turned round to have a look; the bed was piled high with options! It was times like this that I missed the big wardrobe I use to own in my old house. Lots of space for beautiful clothes, and they were mirrored too, so you could get a good feel of how you looked. Sadly they had never been filled with those beautiful clothes I craved, and I never looked in the mirrors that much either... the mirror was something I often hid from at that time in my life. oh well, that is what it is, and now I am dealing with a smaller space for the beautiful clothes I'd finally been able to buy myself. I would then check myself out in the one THIN full-length mirror I owed. Would I really change what I had now for what I had then I asked myself? No was the answer, not if it meant living the rest of my life as a lie. I was finally starting to see the effort, the hurt both emotional and physical, even losing my family, it was worth it just to be real for once, just to be true to myself. The way I felt today was the happiest I had ever felt, who cared for a big house if it didn't bring happiness, life was too short, and I wanted to grab happiness whilst it was on offer.

STEVEN JAMES, 8TH AUGUST 9AM

I wasn't sure what I was thinking, or what I was feeling right now. If I was honest, it had all been a bit of a bombshell, a total left hooker in the face and I have been doubting myself and my judgements, and even my life ever since it had hit me. How had I not noticed that she wasn't a normal woman, wasn't even really a woman at all. Was it because I hadn't had that many women before her to be able to compare her with, I wondered, but was I really that unobservant? I kept on asking myself had I slept with a man? But I didn't think so, she was all woman in certain areas that much I did know. Everything had seemed as it should when we were naked together. There were definitely woman parts, I wasn't that blind. The only clue, as far as I could tell, was a slight scarring under her breasts, where I'd presumed, she'd had breast enhancement surgery. I never asked her about it, as I'd thought that was rude. I always assumed she'd tell me about it one day if she felt the need…. Well, I'd certainly found out about it in the end. I guess it was embarrassment that I was feeling, and very hurt.

Generally, I didn't like to use the word 'normal' as a descriptive word as it was so open to interpretation, what was 'normal' anyway. I myself had been accused of not being 'normal' in the past by my friends and peers, and it always hurt when I heard it as to me, I was my normal. And here I find myself using that very word I have hated for so long to describe the woman I loved over the last few months. The irony of it was not lost on me. Falling in love with Mia had been the making of me. A lifetime trapped in my own world, in my own head, never feeling like I fully fitted in anywhere, being slightly out of kilter with the world and the people around me. Meeting Mia had changed all of that, I felt like I was finally joining in with the world. I know people thought I was a little odd, I could hear them talking about me, or whispering in the kitchen at work when they thought I wasn't about, they thought I couldn't hear, they thought I didn't have feelings. That moment when a room goes silent when you walk in, that was a familiar experience for me. Always had been. My childhood mates were great though, they would put me in my place, but I know even they thought I was a little odd. 'Socially awkward' that's what they would say about me, and I'd never really known what they had meant by that. Still don't think I really do, but I can see where they were coming from with the implication. But with Mia I never felt socially awkward when I was with her, she never made me feel like that, even if that's what other people saw. I felt like I belonged in the world when I was with her. Now I felt like I was back to square one with life.

It was strange. She obviously use to be a man. She told me. But was she really a woman now, I just didn't know? It was a subject I knew very little about, it wasn't something that had ever touched my life before. I don't think I feel angry she hadn't told me she use to be a man right from the outset of us meeting, I think I feel confused more than anything. I've sat and thought about it, and done some research on the subject, and none of what I have read ties in with Mia, the woman I have fallen for. I don't think I understand the logistics of how it all happened, and the process someone has to follow through with to make this 'change' a reality, and I don't know that I'll ever understand the reason behind why someone would do that to themselves. Why someone would feel that way, I just didn't know. But even with all this confusion I have, and the questions I want answers to, I am still missing her madly. I'm missing talking to her, seeing her, enjoying her company and having a laugh with her. I'm desperate to pick the phone up and call her, just to hear her voice at the other end of the line. I have a million questions, but I don't feel I can ask her any of them. I'm giving myself an enforced break, some space from her and this situation. I need to make sure any decision I make about our relationship is the right one for me, long term, and is not just some knee jerk reaction because I am lonely and want to wind the clock back to before I knew. That's how I had run my entire life, it was a formula that had protected me for many years, and it was a formula I would apply to the now, no matter how hard it was. Take my time. The thing that made me the saddest though in all of this sad situation was the thought of her son. Her poor little boy who no longer had a dad to look up too. The thought of that poor little lad feeling alone, feeling abandoned, feeling the way I had felt when I was a young lad, it broke my heart, and I didn't even know him. I felt so sorry for him, for the path that lay ahead of him, the years can be cruel without your parents. I know I felt angrier about that side of things over any feelings of my own that may have been hurt during the process. Could I put that situation in a box, deal with it and file it away and move on? That was a question I just couldn't answer right now, but I hope the answer would come to me soon. I felt lonely, but I'd spent most of my life feeling lonely. That was an easier emotion to deal with today, and for the foreseeable future. I knew what I was doing with lonely.

OLIVER

I loved my mum so much, she was all I had left in this world, but she sometimes really annoys me still, like today, she's really annoying me today. It was days like today that I really missed my dad. Not that he was around that much before he died, I don't think I ever lived with him, and he didn't come over to see me that much, but I still liked having him about, to be able to call him if I wanted to or something. My mum doesn't like to talk about what happened to him. She wouldn't even let me go to the funeral. She said it would be too much for me to deal with and she didn't want me getting upset on my own, and she didn't want to go with me. But I wish I had gone. It might have made it feel real, as it doesn't feel real to me at all. I still keep thinking dad will pop round to see me, turn up with a new toy for me like he did, take me out on my bike, or out somewhere exciting for the day, but he doesn't. It makes me feel different at school too, that my dad had died. All the other kids talk about their dads and what they have been up too, and I can't. Mum said not to tell my friends at school he even died as it might make the other kids sad, so I don't. I wish I could though.

I sneak downstairs to use the house phone. I'm not allowed a mobile phone, even though all the other kids at school have one. It's so unfair. Mum says I don't need one and she can't afford one, now dad isn't about to help she doesn't get any money, so we have to be careful. But she buys stuff for herself which I don't understand. She doesn't like me calling my nan either, my

191

dad's mum, so I wait until she is out the way to call my nan. I like calling nan, she always tells me lots of stories about my dad, funny things he would get up to as a kid and stuff. I think my nan misses him lots too, I think she likes to tell me the stories as it makes her happy to remember things. It makes me happy too. It makes me feel like he is still here, and I like that, I don't care what my mum says. The phone just rang and rang today though which was annoying. Nan must be out, maybe with her friends. And Grandad is always out so I know he won't answer the phone. I don't mind that though, he can be a bit grumpy and isn't as fun to talk too anyway. He doesn't like to tell me stories about dad, even if I ask him. I feel like he doesn't want me around, and can't be bothered to talk to me. I feel like he doesn't even like dad, I hear him tutting when I ask about dad. I feel really sad now as I know I won't get the chance to call nan for another couple of days, and I was really wanting to hear her stories today, to make me feel happy. I really wanted to hear about my dad and the time he got stuck up a tree and his brothers were all joking with him about it. I wanted to hear that story more than anything. Mum caught me climbing a tree today, she told me off and has grounded me, and that's why I'm annoyed with her. I know it's because she cares, she tells me that all the time, but she made me look like a silly kid in front of my friends, and right now I'm so annoyed with her and I don't want to talk to her. She's gone back to work now, and told the other mums I'm not allowed out. It's the school holidays, and I'm stuck in the house when all my friends are outside. Nan would have understood, nan would have laughed about me climbing up the tree, and made me feel better about being stuck in doors now. I wish she wasn't out; I really need her today.

I go to my bedroom and pull out the secret box I have hidden under my bed. I know mum can't find it here, I have hidden it really well. Inside the box I have some pictures that I like to look at when I am feeling sad, they always help cheer me up a little. There is a picture of me and my dad together on a day out somewhere, I can't remember where we were but that doesn't really matter. In the picture I can see I look a little bit like him, we have the same hair colour and our eyes look the same. He looks all nice in his best shirt, and I am in a matching one he brought for me. I was only little in the picture, I don't even remember it being taken, but the picture makes me remember him, remember his smell and his voice and how strong he felt when he held my hand. It always made me feel safe when he held my hand, safe and proud, proud to be looked after and loved by him. Looking at the picture now makes me feel like I will see him soon. I never want that feeling to go away ever. It gives me hope that one day it may come true, that he may come and see me again, and that he hasn't really died.

STEVEN JAMES, 10TH SEPTEMBER 5PM

It had been several weeks now since I'd seen Mia, or even spoken to her. For all I knew she may have moved on to someone else already, leaving me a distance blip in her memory. It was the thought of that that made me come too, realising I needed to man up about it. I was going to contact her today, I needed to, for me. Whatever the outcome might be I needed to speak to her, ask my questions, and take in her responses. Only then would I be able to move on with my life, in whatever form that might be. She might hate me for walking away and taking all this time, or she might be willing to talk me through it. I wasn't sure what way it was going to go. Two months ago I'd have said Mia was a very understanding lady who wouldn't shirk away her responsibilities, and would have been open to me asking questions, but given what I had found out I wasn't so sure about that side of her anymore. Maybe she would run away and hide from me, now I know the truth. Maybe she never wanted me to know the truth all along. But I did know now, and I can't carry on like this anymore. I'm a coward though, I couldn't face seeing her just yet, I didn't want to risk falling into her arms and forgiving all before I have had answers to my questions, and let her know how I am really feeling. I decided that an old school pen and paper letter was the best way to approach her. So I sat down to write:

'Dear Mia

Firstly I need to apologies to you for not being in contact with you sooner. There are no excuses for just leaving you like that, no matter what you have done I should have stayed and talked it through with you. Secondly, before I go any further with this, I need you to know just how hurt I am that you lied to me. This is massive, you should have told me right from the start. And thirdly, I'm sorry I can't do this in person just yet, hence why I have taken to writing to you. You need to give me time and space with this, but you do own me some answers. Or maybe you don't owe me anything, after the way I left you, you may have moved on already for all I know.

Sorry, that was harsh Mia. I hope that I am wrong, and that I meant more to you than that, that I wasn't just some fling that you could easily walk away from. I know you meant more to me than that, and I think that is why I am feeling so hurt about you lying to me. I had fallen for you Mia in a big way and I could see a future expanding ahead for us together. I guess what I would like from you now is some information about what has happened to you, and why it has happened. That may be a tough one to answer, but I would like you to try please. If we are to stand any chance in the future I need to have a full understanding of what you have gone through, and why. I hope you understand that, and if your feelings for me were genuine. I hope you offer me the respect of answering those questions at least.

I'm not saying I don't love you anymore, as I do Mia. You changed my life for the better that day we met. I couldn't believe my luck that day, when we finally met in person, I thought you was amazing, and I found you so easy to talk to. I thought you found me easy to talk to too, but I must have presented you with some barriers for you not to have been able to tell me the truth from the start, for that I am truly sorry. Would we have carried on from that point, I don't know, and I guess we never will? But we did carry on, with one of us knowing the truth, and one of us not, and in that time, I fell in love with you Mia. That now makes this revelation of yours harder to just walk away from, as I am in too emotionally involved with you to just walk away and forget it ever happened. For some people they might think we were only together a few months so what's the stress, but for me that time seemed far longer, and more meaningful than just a few months. Is that how you saw it? Or did I read that all wrong too?

I guess what I am saying is that I need some time to get my head around the situation, I need to get my head around the fact that I have fallen in love with someone who use to be a man, just like me. I need to be able to see past that fact to be able to see the woman I know you really are. I have read up a lot on the subject in the last few weeks Mia, and I get you have probably always been a woman trapped in that man's body, but my head isn't quite there with it all yet. This might be something you have been living with forever, but it only just landed in my life just over a month ago. I'm a slow burner with stuff at the best of times, this is going to take me some time to understand, and adjust too. I hope you are willing to help me, but I'll understand if you don't.

I do hope I meant something to you though Mia, that you weren't just using me to experiment with. And I hope you can find it in your heart to write back to me when you are ready, hopefully with some answers to my questions. Please don't call me yet, I'm not ready for that, if you don't mind. I need to be able to read you answers and re-read them back as many times as I need to, so that I fully understand what you are saying, and where you are at, if that makes sense. It's what will work best for me. I'll let you know when I am ready to talk.

I hate this, I really do. I hate feeling hurt and I hate still loving you. It would be easier to be able to just walk away, but I can't. I'll await your response, Mia.

Regards

Steven.'

I didn't put a kiss at the end of the letter, I didn't feel like it, that sort of felt wrong given the circumstances. I had poured my heart out onto the paper, something I could never do in a face-to-face situation, and I had told her I still loved her, but a kiss, no, I needed to hold something back for myself, just in case I was totally wrong about her and she had just been using me. I stuffed the letter into an envelope, stuck a first class stamp on in and took it straight to the post box at the end of my street before I could change my mind about sending it. I had to move on one way or the other, and that letter now encased by the solid red post box could be the key. I hope so anyway.

MIA, 8TH OCTOBER

I sat on the sea wall, my legs dangling down and hanging freely as if I were a child again. My feet were not able to reach and touch the sand beneath me. Childhood, that time in life when everything around you was big and safe, when every experience seemed to offer you a freedom that's never to be experienced again, only you don't realise that at the time. You'd be caught in the moment of whatever is going on around you, keen to move onto the next adventure, time was an easy thing to waste back then. That was a long distant memory now, another lifetime ago, and another life altogether for me. The sea was rolling in with force now, the turn of the tide giving it strength and momentum, the sea almost getting carried away with itself, folding in on itself again and again. The waves were crashing down on the beach as if with a mission, their sound almost crying out to those that were listening that it didn't want to stop, and it wouldn't be told too either. The waves did have a mission I guess… and that mission was evolution. They played their part in everything around us, constantly changing the grains of sand they smashed themselves against so heavily, their aim to make smaller grains, or different shaped grains. The landscape constantly changes around us over the years, and the sea plays its part in that change too. Entire sections of the British coastline had given way to the forces of water, never to be the same again, the change permanent and at times unforgiving to the lives it destroys in its wake. I'd come a long way myself, with changing, and evolving, and like the coastline, there was no going back for me either. I had been smashed against the rocks too many times, so to speak, and had come out the other side a different person, in more ways than just the physical effects people could see. The salt-tinged spray was reaching my legs now, every third of fourth wave coating me in its fresh and salty water. I love the sea when it is like this. It's its own boss, no one can tell it what to do, no one can stop it, it will take whatever path it chooses too. Most people stayed away from the sea's edge on days like today, for fear of getting wet, or being swept away, preferring the calmer days for playing on the beach and eating an ice cream with the kids. For me though, this was the best kind of day to see the sea, the only kind of day to sit and really take it all in. Nature at its best, wild and free, a bit like me. The sounds of the crashing waves were blocking out the nagging fears in my head, that second person we all have inside of us that chats away to you, motivating you along, or putting you down. I felt at ease with myself, and a peace descended upon me, I didn't want my head chatter ruining the moment for me. I could feel my body relaxing for the first time in a long time and I wanted to embrace it. I was a new me, but I was still me, the me I had been since the day I arrived on this planet. Mia had been trapped inside of me all along, and I didn't have space for anyone from my past who couldn't accept and embrace that fact. How could I, that alone could destroy me, and I had been through too much to do that to myself anymore.

We were getting on okay now, Steven and I. He had written to me, and I had written back, as he had asked me too. Since then things have started to improve between us. We probably had a way to go though, before we can go back to where we were before it all came out. I can't complain, I have no right to complain, given how I have treated him. I hadn't been honest with him from the start, and I was very lucky he was still even talking to me. I'm not sure I'd have been as forgiving if the boot had been on the other foot. Everything had been a whirlwind around me at the time, and my change from a man's body I didn't want, to a female's body that I did want, it had all blown my mind a little, that reality that I could be me for the first time in my life. But that was no excuse for not being honest with anyone, let alone someone I was falling in love with. That hiding had become so ingrained in my being that sometimes I didn't know I was even doing it. I had been protecting myself for years with lies, and it had taken falling in love, and nearly losing that love to snap me out of it, to grow up, and start treating people with the respect that they deserved. It was a two-way street; I know that now.

I'd come away for a few days by myself, for myself, something I should have done a long time ago. To breath the fresh air of Southwold deep into my soul, to find this new me a little bit, to get to know myself again, now I'm out in the open for the first time I needed to take some time out for me. I love this place, always have, it's like stepping back in time and walking into a calmer world coming here. I have lots of fond memories of this small town that had somehow managed to escape the modern make over a lot of seaside towns are burdened with, today I was making some more memories for myself. On this cold October weekend there weren't that many people about but that really suited me just fine. I just wanted some space from people. I don't want to engage in idle chit chat right now, I just want to look at the sea, and have space to breath.

Steven and I had agreed we'd take our relationship, our friendship, one step at a time for now. We'd take the time to get to know each other all over again. Start from afresh. No more lies. It was very brave of him to even consider giving me anything, most men wouldn't have offered me that I'm sure, in fact, I know they wouldn't have. I lump the old me into that too. Steven had said he wanted to get to know the real Mia, the bits I had been hiding. He called it hiding, not lying, I think he was being very kind with his words. But he wanted to know it all, the why's, how's and all the emotional stuff in-between. And I couldn't blame him an ounce for that. I think Steven had had a troubled life, or a rough start some would say. I think I need to get to re-know him too, there is a lot more to him that is hidden behind his face, more than he is letting onto, but I believe it's all good qualities. I wouldn't have been so upset about him leaving otherwise. I know without a shadow of doubt that this is the man I want to share my life with, he just needs to be able to understand me first, to be able to love me again, to see if the real unhidden me was someone he wanted to love again and share his life with too. All I could hope for was that once he had gotten to know the real me, that I was that someone he wanted to love again.

It was the end of my weekends escape from real life and was time to leave the safety of this seaside town and head home and face the music. I didn't mind the thought of the drive ahead, and as I set off the roads were nice and clear. It was probably the time of year that had something to do with it as there wasn't a car to be seen on the winding narrow lane, meandering through idyllic villages, with a vast expanse of countryside in-between one village and the next. This was idyllic to people like me, maybe not so much to the people living here, always having a trek when they needed something or on heavier traffic days when they were trying to get to work. Mind you, my town was fast being swallowed up by new builds and large factories, the countryside fast disappearing to a distant memory. On a day like today I would swap my busy town for this peace and quiet, no matter how isolating it may be. But I probably wouldn't fit in with the locals, if they guessed what I was, or was that just me being presumptuous and not giving people the chance??

The break to Southwold had done me the world of good though, I felt relaxed and happy, and most importantly I felt at one with myself. That was something money couldn't buy, it was something that had to come from within you. What would be would be for anything out of my control. For everything else I did have a choice. I could choose to go out and make new friends, I could choose to better myself career wise. I had good skills, I had chosen not to carry on with that career option, maybe I was cutting off my own nose to spite my face, and only I could do something about that. It was down to me, and no one else, only I could make the change for me. There was nothing stopping me going back into my old career, noting except me. So what if it was a male dominated environment, so what if there would be some ribbing. That's all it would be, ribbing, banter, jolliness. I had held my own for many years in the industry and environment and the way I felt today I could hold my own there again, ribbing and banter and all. It was time I faced a lot of things, and as nice as my current job was, I needed to challenge my brain again, I needed to do what I was good as, and not worry about the gender dominance anymore.

That thought process alone had taken up nearly two hours of my journey. I seemed to be driving my well-practiced route on auto pilot whilst sorting out the final pieces of the jigsaw puzzle that made up my life, I was enjoying myself in a funny way. I think I had finally got to a place where I could be as happy as any person was. I wasn't silly enough to think life would be a complete bed of roses all the time, that would be naïve of me. But I could achieve better than I had been doing recently, that was for sure. A more honest approach had the potential for happiness with longevity. Who would want anything else?

It wasn't long before I reached home and was pulling my car into my street, the end of my driven journey and the start of the journey of the rest of my life. My little home was sat at the end of the road, the sun was shining down on it almost making it stand out within my street, the light bouncing off my clean windows, it couldn't look more perfect in my eyes. It was my place of safety, my own space to be me, behind a closed door, and out in the open. My little house was the place I had learnt to be me, the place where I had learnt about Mia, a castle that had served me better than anywhere else I had lived before, it was one thing I had no intention of changing. I couldn't see me moving from here for a long time. But wat I wasn't expecting to see was anyone knocking on my front door, or not anyone I knew that is. If I'd been pushed to guess, I might have thought that Steven may have visited me, but why would he?! He was so black and white about life and stuff in general, he wasn't one to turn up unannounced when he had said he needed time to think and get use to things. Unannounced just wasn't in his nature. He would contact me first, and his contact would be via e-mail, or text, the safe electronical style, so as not to rock the complicated systems that seem to operate in his brain, that much I could see and knew. So apart from Steven I was not expecting anyone else I knew to be knocking on my front door. The slim female figured turned to look as I parked my car. My jaw dropped, and I nearly crashed into the neighbour's car, I slammed on the brakes. There stood my mother!

Everything went fuzzy and cloudy. I gripped the steering wheel even though I was no longer moving anywhere. I took a couple of deep breaths before I stepped out of the car. In that short time I had run through why she might be here, at my door. Maybe my father had died, or perhaps one of my brothers had been in an accident or something. I Couldn't really see any other reason she would be here, or even how she had found me in the first place!

'Hello Michael.' She spoke. The name stabbing through my heart like someone trying to kill me. I tried not to get annoyed, her face was soft, and she was half smiling at me. She wasn't here in anger so why should I be angry.

'Hello Mum.' I replied with a voice I knew she wouldn't have known, far softer than Michael's, I don't know that I would recognise his voice now anyway.

'Can we go indoors love?' She asked, I could sense she was a little nervous, and trying not to show her shock at the difference in me, her Michael, her son.

'Of Course.' I stepped past her as I was fumbling trying to find my keys. I found them at the bottom of my handbag. 'Come in.' I gestured. 'Have you been waiting long? Can I get you a drink?'

'Not too long love, and that would be nice, I'll have a coffee if you have one.' She replied, our 'welcome' routine the same as it always had been, like I had only seen her yesterday, not several years ago.

I made us both a cup of coffee and we sat down on the sofa, side by side, the kitchen table had too much stuff piled on it and I couldn't be bothered to move it all right now. I know she would have preferred to be sat at the table, and she'd have also preferred me to still be her son. There was a lot she would have to just roll with today.

'Mum…. You do know I'm Mia now, don't you? I'm a full woman, almost the same as you.' I had to get it out there in the open before it became a subject we just danced around, like many things had been danced around before with my mother. As long as everything looked OK from the outside she was happy to dance.

'I know love, I can see that.' She pursed her lips; it made her look like she had just been stung by a wasp. 'But to me you will always be my Michael, and my son. I gave birth to you, I raised you, and I miss you, son.' She paused; I think to stop herself from crying.

I'm not going to lie, I missed her too, dreadfully, but she was really hurting me with her non-acceptance of who I really was. I held her hand and took a moment, the comfort from her touch giving me the strength to continue.

'Mum… I've missed you so much too. I have had to do this all on my own' I gestured to my body. 'And I can tell you now mum, it's been a long and lonely journey.' She looked down at her feet, I could see she felt some level of guilt at leaving her child to cope with this alone, albeit a grown up one, but who doesn't need their mum in their hour of need, no matter how old we are.

'I'm here because I want to be part of your life Michael. I'm here because the pain of not seeing you is too much to deal with anymore. Your father… well… I'm sad to say he won't have any of it, but you know what he's like. But me, well, I'm different, and I can't carry on without seeing you, knowing that you are OK. I want to be able to pick up the phone and call you just to see how your day has been.'

'You don't know how much that means to me Mum. But I am Mia now and not Michael. My voice has changed, as you can hear. My body has changed beyond recognition, and I have changed too. Do you think you can accept Mia into your life mum, to embrace having a daughter now, to pick up the phone to me and hear my new voice?' It had to be said. As much as I missed her, I couldn't live in a lie anymore, not now, I'd come too far, and I didn't want to let her back in to only be hurt again.

'To be honest ' she paused 'Now I am sat here with you I don't know if I can love, I really don't. It's so hard seeing you like this, it's a lot to take in love.'

The words stung like a slap to the face… to have her sat here in my safe place and take that feeling away, to have to deal with her leaving me all over again…. That would just be too cruel. I wished she'd never come to find me now, I was okay three hours ago, why did she come just to do this to me. We sat in silence for what felt like an age, still holding onto each other's hands, but not making any eye contact or speaking any words. I think she was trying to feel for Michael, feel her son, to see if he was still there somehow. I let her as I hoped she could feel me, as me was still in there, it didn't matter what the outside shell displayed, or what my name was, I was still part of her.

'I don't know if I can love. I really don't.' She paused. 'But I am willing to try, for you.' She risked looking into my eyes, hers were clearly watery, this was as big a thing for her as it was for me.

'Thank you.' Was all I could say, no more words were needed as I fought back the tears. I let her hold me in her arms, I let her hold me like I was six years old again. I realised now that I can cope in life without my dad, he never really got me anyway, and we'd never really enjoyed a relationship, but I needed my mum in my life now more than ever.

Would she stop calling me Michael, the name she had chosen for me, her first born chid. Only time would tell if that was something she could cope with. Rome wasn't built in a day so they say, I think one step at a time is the best plan of action I could have at the moment with lots of aspects of my life. She was willing to try, and she was here, and that went a long way in my books. I needed to be a little bit flexible too. If the odd 'Michael' slipped out of her mouth I needed to learn to not jump down her throat about it. I had her back in my life, and that was the most important thing to me, and perhaps always had been. As for the rest of it, only time would tell really, but I felt sure I would be able to tackle whatever may be thrown in my direction.

MIA, 12TH OCTOBER 9PM

I got in from work late today, I'd been for a drink with the girls after work which had been really nice. I'd felt relaxed, and not on edge, and it had taken my mind off of my mother's visit a few days pervious. We had had a nice chat and laugh about some of the things that had gone on in the office lately and I really felt like I was part of the team, finally one of them. I had thoroughly enjoyed the evening and was so glad I'd gone along. Now I'm home, content and armed with a takeaway, ready to crash on the sofa with a bit of light-hearted TV. I grabbed the post from the floor door where it had crash landed. I flicked through to see if there was anything of interest aside from bills. A handwritten envelope commanded my attention, I dropped everything else back on the floor. The envelope had my mother's distinctive curvy handwriting and the envelope was addressed to Mia. I walked over to the sofa. I sat down whilst staring at the envelope, hoping this wasn't a letter telling me that she had had a change of heart and no longer wanted a relationship with me after all. I was nervous about opening it, but I forced myself to do just that. Folding open the letter and smoothing it down, delaying starting reading it I braced myself for what was ahead. Finally, I let my eyes focus on the words...

Dear Son

The day you were born was totally and utterly life changing for me. I can remember I held you in my arms in total awe of you, and you'd only been in the world a few minutes. You were so small, and so perfect, and suddenly nothing else mattered in the world except you. Not even your father could come close to the love I felt for you. I looked down at your perfect face as I held you in my arms, your beautiful eyes demanding my sole attention, then you scrunched your little face up and had a big yawn. My first-born boy, I couldn't have been prouder at that moment, and I didn't even know you yet. You hadn't done anything in the world yet for me to be proud of, but proud is how I was feeling at that moment. Maybe I was proud of myself a bit too, for giving birth to such a perfect baby boy, my biggest achievement and mark on the world, previously living in you fathers' shadows, you were something I had created, carried, and given life too. In that one moment I wanted the whole world for you, and I wanted to protect you in my arms forever, safe, content, and just you and me. I also wanted you to become a successful man, find love, and never experience sadness, it was such a mixture of feelings and emotions at that moment I thought I would explode with it all but the strongest feeling I had was that I never wanted that day to end, that first day with you, that day where everything was ahead of us as a family, as mother and son. If I could have frozen time still, I would have frozen it at that very moment. A time I could keep you safe and protect you from the big wide world yet have hopes and dreams for you at the same time. I knew back then I wanted to be able to keep you as a baby, when all your choices were mine to make. Funnily, when your brothers came along in the following years I never felt quite as strongly about keeping them little and not letting anyone else in, I was the total opposite, I looked forward to them growing a bit and being able to do things for themselves. I love you all fiercely the same, but there was something a lot stronger with you, my first-born baby boy.

The years started to fly by far too quickly for my liking. At seven years old you were such a sweet boy, yet I didn't know where seven years had gone! You had such a caring nature and way about you it was lovely to watch you developing and grow. I'd see you helping other children in the playground, picking up the ones who fell over and cried, or being the mediator if two kids wanted to play fight. By then I'd become a helper at dinner times at your school just so I could be near you and your brothers and protect you if you had been bullied, or just there for you if you needed me. I never needed to worry about that though really, everyone loved you, you seemed to be everyone's favourite friend and all the kids wanted to know you. It was nice for me though, to be able to share this part of your life from afar, and I'd been lucky that your dad didn't need me to work a regular paid job, he earnt good enough money to support us all, so my focus could be fully on raising you and your brothers. I didn't think I'd been different with you to how I was with your brothers, but maybe I was, I don't know. Your gentle ways were the same when we had your friends' round to the house to play. You were always fussing around making sure your friends were happy and enjoying themselves, almost at the expense of your own happiness, like a proper little host would do. I could see myself in you and I liked that shared trait we had. I always liked to make sure guests were happy no matter what, your father complained to me about it all the time as it often meant I didn't enjoy the night myself. You never seemed to mind sharing your toys with your brothers, or your friends either. I took this as a good quality for your future. I couldn't say the same about your brothers, they hated sharing anything and would fight all the time over who touched this or that. They were always rolling around the floor fighting about something, but you seemed gentler than them in a way, I could never put my finger on it, but it didn't matter then, I loved your nature just the way it was. You shouldn't have favourites with your children, and I would never admit this to anyone for fear of people thinking I was a bad mother, but you was always my favourite boy, my favourite child. No matter how hard I tried to change that I just couldn't. You was the one that was always first to my mind. I loved your brothers, of course I did, but there was just something about you that drew me in and kept me there. I loved being in your company, and just being with you all the time if I could. I think it annoyed your father a little, I think he felt pushed out, but I didn't care.

As time moved on you grew and made more friends. We would always have friends to the house and you always seemed to get more fun out of watching your friends playing with your toys than you ever did when you were playing with those toys yourself. You seemed to know I liked the house to be kept tidy too and would be the child that cleared up and put the toys away when you or your friends had finished playing with them, as opposed to your brothers who left things where they were, abandoned without a care in the world. It would drive me mad at the time, that they weren't more like you. I didn't understand how you could all be so different from one another, you came from the same two parents, surly your genetic makeup and personalities would be the same?!

The years rumbled on and family life with the three of you around always seemed so busy. As you all got older there wasn't time to think too much about things, I just seemed to lurch from one commotion to the next. I just had to get on with looking after the three of you, the washing alone seemed like a full-time job. Then there were clubs to get you all to, football training, rugby training for your brothers, scouts, exams to get you all to revise for, the list was never ending and your social life at that time was far better than mine! But I have to say it was always good fun and I loved it, and I loved being needed. You father was a good man but thinking back now it was about that time that he started to become a little distant from us all. I think he found the stress of three teenage boys in the house a bit too much to deal with, all that puberty and the hormones pushed him into finding his own clubs where he could be with men of his own age. He would take your bothers with him sometimes, when I'd complain that he didn't do much with any of you, but you never seemed to want to go along, and your father never seemed to push you to go along either. Its only now I think back I wonder if that's where it all started. There was without a shadow of doubt a lack of something between the two of you. It wasn't a lack of love; I know that much, but there was a lack of something. Your father would tell me how much he loved you, and I could see in his eye he was genuine with his love for you. He just didn't seem to be able to connect with you in the same way as he did with your brothers, in a way that made for a lasting meaningful relationship. Just saying you love someone doesn't make for a relationship, there has to be something else behind the words. It broke my heart for you, and I think I over compensated and loved you even more because of how your father was with you. It didn't seem to bother you though, or rather you didn't seem to notice how he was, and you seemed happy to be at home with me whilst your brothers were out with your father.

Then we hit the years when you boys all started bringing girls home to the house and I quite liked it. The girls seemed to bring and extra buzz to the house and all the excitement gave me a new lease of life. Secretly I had always wanted a daughter, someone who would want to do the girly things with me, someone to be in the same corner as me in such a male dominated house. Your girlfriends gave me someone new I could fuss over, and what girl doesn't like to be fussed over. You boys didn't seem to like being fussed over so much as you'd got older, except you, if your brothers weren't around, you'd still let me fuss over you. The girls you all met seemed to calm you all down a bit too, which I felt was a good thing. Well that's how it seemed to me, your mum, anyway. You never seemed to settle with any one girl though, I just thought you wanted to make sure you picked the right one for marriage and all that before you committed. And they were all nice girls, the ones I met, you had very good taste in woman

Michael. They were all very good with me too, always making time to get to know me. I think the girls could see how close you and I were, and to win you over they would need to win me over too. Except Oliver's Mum, she was a bit different of course, we've spoken about her many times before so I won't go over that old ground now, but she seemed to be on a mission right from the start, woman to woman I could see that, something you men sometimes miss. She had no time for me then, and still has no time for me now, even though I am her son's grandmother. I felt so angry at the time, when she fell pregnant with Oliver, she used you so badly and I could see the hurt she that she caused you and that hurt me. Of course, I never told you that at the time, I didn't want to interfere too much and cause you anymore pain. I just held you when you needed to be held and listened when you needed someone to talk too. You always struck me as someone who would want to do it all the right way, marriage first, and then the kids. I often wondered if you would propose to her after she fell pregnant, and then when Oliver arrived, but the more I got to know her I could see that was never her intention with you, she didn't love you as much as you didn't love her and she never wanted to be married to you or share a life with you. But then we got Oliver, and how could I remain angry with her when she gave me such a beautiful Grandson. You were always so good with him too, a complete natural when it came to parenting when you were allowed to see him, which always seemed a bit hit and miss to me, no real routine to it which is hard for a child. But it was what it was, and we always made Oliver feel loved when we did get to see him.

I wouldn't have said you was close to your brothers when you were little, they seemed like a tight knit little boy unit and close, like brothers should be, and you seemed pushed out somehow. Or maybe you just didn't push yourself in and join in with them, I don't know then and I still don't know why it was like that. It sometimes made me feel sad for you, but then again life was so busy back then that feeling would soon pass as I had to deal with the next thing thrown my way. But I had noticed that the three of you all became a lot closer when you hit late teens and early twenties. I was pleased, and so was your father, but I couldn't help feeling that the bond between you and them still wasn't as strong as the bond they had between themselves. You didn't seem bothered by it, so I tried not to let the niggle worry me, and they did seem to try to let you join in with their boys' nights out a bit more. I just got the feeling you went along to be with them, but that the boy's nights out were not really your thing. Maybe I'm looking back with too much hindsight, or maybe I have always just worried about you too much. Who knows.

I've never stopped loving you son, not for one minute. The day you told me about what had been going on inside of you my world fell apart. I felt like I had failed you and that I had failed as a mother, and I knew this was something your father was going to struggle to take in. He was such a proud man, how would he explain this to his friends at his various clubs, the thing that seems to matter most to him in this world, it was something I don't think he could do then, and sadly I don't think he'll ever be able to tell anyone about you, I'm sorry to say. And that was a little bit how I felt, at first, I am very ashamed to say. I'd been proud of you from day one, and now I had to explain to all my friends I no-longer had a number one son, I now had a daughter. It's a really hard thing to explain to people. I didn't know how I could do that and still hold my head high. I felt like our life together had all been a lie and that you had hated every second of anything we had done together as mother and son, and that really broke my heart. I just wanted it all to go away, I wanted to turn back the clock, all the way back to the day you were born, to hold you in my arms once again, and maybe raise you a different way, maybe change this outcome, maybe be a better mother to you.

But then I did some reading, on the internet. I know that may seem strange to you, but I've got a tablet now and I love it for reading the news, and stuff like that. Anyway, I found this website that helped people like me, mums of people who make the same 'change' that you have. Well, it's not just mums on there, there's dads on there too, and other close relatives and even people's friends. They have a thing on there, I think they call it a chat room?? It's been wonderful, I can chat to people so openly on there, there is no shame, just support for each other, and it's really easy to use too. And what with it being on my tablet, your father doesn't need to know I'm doing it and talking to people about what you have done, he would hit the roof if he knew I have to be honest. He doesn't trust anything like that and he doesn't like me talking to people about what happened with you. Anyway, as well as being able to chat to other people in my position, there is lots of formal information on there to read too. I've found it both hard to read, and quite sad too. I'm sad for the life we have lost together, but mostly I am sad that you felt so trapped like that and for so long too. I feel ashamed that I had barriers up leaving you feeling like you couldn't talk to me about it. I know, I wouldn't have been approachable about it back then, or I wouldn't have to be writing this letter now, and that makes me very sad too, that I have behaved like that to you, my number one child, the one I would have walked over hot coals for. Easy words to say, an action I didn't follow through with. I have a lot of thinking to do myself now, as a mother, and as a human being too.

Seeing you the other day was like seeing you for the first time all over again, only you're too big now for me to hold in my arms and keep safe. I want to have a relationship with you again, I really do, I don't think I can carry on without you in my life in some form or another, I hope you want me back in your life again too? I know it may take time for us to rebuild some trust again between us, and get to know each other again, but I hope you can let me back in to your life and have a parent child relationship with me once again. I'm not going to lie, starting again as grownups of the same sex is not going to be easy, for either of us, not like when you were a baby boy and I was the adult. We have to start again with some things I know, for starters I now have that daughter I always wanted to go shopping with. I just hope I'm not to use to scuttling about the shops on my own now to be able to enjoy that with you. And I do want to try and enjoy shopping with you. But you, the person I raised, you are still in there, Mia, Michael, the name doesn't matter, and shouldn't matter, its what's inside that counts, and it's our relationship that matters the most to me. Your personality and sense of humour are still there, and I miss them, and I miss you. And there is no shame in still talking about the shared memories we have, that's what they said on the chat room. Things like holidays we've been on, Christmases, funny things you did as a child, we still shared that moment in time after all and I hope you are okay if I want to talk about them with you sometimes.

I'm sorry I never said all this the other day when I saw you. I found it all quite hard to take in, harder than I thought it would be. I think I lost my tongue a bit, unlike me I know! Look love. Your father, he may never understand what has happened, it's not in his make up to take new things on easily, especially with something so alternative. That's how he would see it anyway. And your brothers, they are too like their dad for their own good and it saddens me they never talk about you, or not around me they don't. I hope they still care for you, and with them being of a younger generation I'm hoping that in time they will come around and can at least talk to you or be in the same room as you so we can all be together sometimes, a mother and all her children. That would mean the world to me. If I can try to understand what has happened to you, I would like to think there is a little bit of genetics of me in them and that they try to understand too. We can only hope my love. Give it time.

One last thing, and I have to be very honest, I can't promise it's going to be easy for me to call you Mia all the time, the odd Michael may slip out from time to time, but some of that will be old habits and a slip of the tongue if you know what I mean. I just hope you can forgive me for how I have treated you my darling and let me back into your life as I would very much like to get to know you, my daughter.

Love you always.

Mum xxx

Mum's letter slipped from my hand and landed on the floor besides me. I had a feeling of happiness bouncing around me, and the room felt lighter somehow. Was this the feeling one gets when you feel content? I think I was content; I know I was happy. What a show of strength from my mum. I know it would have taken a lot of inner strength for her to write that letter to me.

You should never regret the things you do, only the things you don't. An interesting statement quoted by many, probably too freely without much thought to the true meaning behind those. Did I regret anything I had done in the last few years? On a good day no I didn't regret anything, not at all. But on a bad day I had to fight that feeling of regret to keep it from bubbling over and spilling out. I regret hurting my family the way I have very much. And I regret losing my friends, but some of that was my own doing outside of my change. That statement was especially true of my friends, I never gave them the chance to reject me and hurt me, I rejected them first. And for that I have massive regrets. I fear there is too much water under the bridge now for me to change, maybe in time, but in all honesty unless a miracle happens, I don't think I want to do anything about it either, having reached the strong point I now find myself in. And if I don't think about them then I don't feel regret. I regret losing my son, robbing him of the father son relationship all his friends will have, but the total loss of me was not my doing, I had to keep that feeling at bay, I just had too. He was safe, fed and I could ensure he always has a roof over his head, from afar.

He is luckier than a lot of kids, I remind myself of that often. Of overall regret though I manage to keep that feeling at bay these days. The question I ask myself in moments of doubt is do I regret becoming the person I should have always been, the person I should have been from birth? And the answer every time is no I don't, not at all. I'm now finally proud of myself, proud that I stood up and spoke out, proud that I did this for myself, and put my mental wellbeing and physical outer shell first. Being a man was slowly killing me, only I didn't really realise that at the time. I could have regrets about the way I handed it all, and how I behaved with those friends I lost and my family, but that's not going to do me any good in the long run. One thing is for sure, you can't turn the clock back and change anything, you have to keep on moving forward. I think the mind has a way of protecting itself and licking its own wounds in times of heightened stress. If I'm busy and getting on with life I almost forget everything that's happened in the past, and I almost forget I was born a man. I'm just getting on with my life as if it has always been this way.

I do regret not being more honest with my new friends, the ones I have made since I became a woman, and that's especially true of Steven, but I can't change that action now either, even if I wanted too. I could only take my own advice and move forward and try to repair the damage I created for myself. I don't regret it, or how I was back then, how can I, I was never being malicious to Steven or anyone else around me at that time, including my parents and my own son. I was only ever doing what I thought was right at a very confusing and difficult time in my life. I was trying to start again, as a woman. Perhaps I should have given myself more time, perhaps I wanted new relationships in my life too quickly, perhaps I wanted them as my sticky plaster to make it all better. Do I really regret that though? I'd have to say no I don't. Steven and I will try to re-build our relationship, I like him a lot, how can I regret him being in my life, if it's meant to be we will get through this. And my work friends, I need to remember that not everyone I encounter in life going forward needs to know my past. As with everyone we meet in life, I don't know all their secrets and we all still get on and have a nice time together. I have learnt from it all though, and I've made new friends who are very important to me because of how I was, and I don't regret them coming into my life one bit. And now my hormone levels are steadier, and my general mental state is the best it's ever been, I've taken it all on board and tried to become a better person for it. Life is a learning curve, and some of us are on a steeper curve than others. What you do with that gained experience is what matters most in life. I don't have space for regret anymore.

OLIVER

I'd been awake for hours, staring at the celling in my bedroom, I just couldn't get back to sleep, I was just too excited. It was like the feeling you get on Christmas Eve when you just want it to be Christmas Day. You know you should go to sleep so you can get to Christmas Day quicker, but you just can't. I just kept rolling around and around in my bed, and now my bedsheets are all tangled around my legs. I knew better than to get up and creep into mums' room and ask if it was nearly time to get up yet. Mum likes her sleep, a lot, and if I wake her too early she'd be grumpy with me all day. I've made that mistake a few times before. Sometimes her grumpy days are okay as it means she doesn't bother me to much or ask me to do stuff around the house, I get left alone in my room, but then other times she'll shout at me lots and nothing I do is right. I don't like those days. But today I don't want to annoy her at all, just in case mum gets really angry with me and changes her mind and doesn't let me go out. I'm sure she wouldn't, I know she loves me as she tells me all the time, but I just don't want to risk it. Today I really can't wait for it to be the day time, and to go out.

I don't get adults sometimes. I don't get why my dad never told me he had a sister before, when he was still alive. He told me lots of things about his life, and I got to see lots of my nan and grandad, and my uncles sometimes when my dad was still alive, but never his sister. And my nan, she never told me I had an

Auntie either, and she told me lots about my family. My mum said it's because dad didn't know that he had a sister, as she was only a half-sister, which sort of made sense, but then I didn't get why he wouldn't know. And if dad didn't know he had a sister, how did my mum know about her? I'd asked mum that very question and she just said that sometimes people might have the same dad but a different mum, and that one day I would understand all that, and that she only just found out herself that I now had an Auntie and not to worry about it all and just enjoy it. I hope she's right and that I do understand it all one day, as right now that all seemed very weird to me. She also told me not to talk to my nan, dad's mum that is, about it all as it would just upset her and drag up the past. I didn't get to see nan so much these days now dad had died, I didn't know when I would see her next anyway, and I wouldn't want to upset her so I promised I wouldn't ask her about my Auntie. Maybe I would ask my other nan, maybe she would be able to explain it to me instead and I saw her all the time. She never seemed to get angry or annoyed about things so I didn't mind asking her stuff. I couldn't wait to meet her though, my new Auntie. I'd never had an Auntie before, only Uncles, and my Uncles didn't seem to like doing much with me so they were pretty boring. I was hoping an Auntie would be a whole lot more fun to be around. My friend at School is always talking about his Auntie, she takes him to loads of exciting places, I hope my Auntie is going to be just like that. I miss my dad so much. When I am on my own I cry when I think about him. He used to do really fun things with me and take me to some really exciting places, and he just let me talk too. He never stopped me or hurried me up or told me I was being silly. I really hope dad's sister is just like him and we get to do lots of fun things together. Mum doesn't seem to have the time to do fun things like that with me, or that's what she says anyway...'We don't have the time this weekend hun... maybe next weekend'...

only the next weekend comes and mum doesn't have the time then either. I know she 'works' all the time to 'keep us going' as she says, but still, I'd like to sometimes do something fun with her too.

I didn't have much more time to wait now, I could hear that mum had finally woken up and was out of bed as her floor was creaking. It was safe for me to leave my room now and go into hers without disturbing her and then we could finally start getting ready. Annoyingly though I now felt tired because I'd been awake for ages already.

'Morning sleepy head' my mum said as she ruffled my hair.

'Morning mum.' I replied as I climbed into her bed whilst she busied about her room, she leant over to kiss me. She did this every morning, except if I had annoyed her.

'Are you excited about meeting your Auntie today?' She asked, she looked a bit excited too.

'I'm so excited mum. I couldn't sleep last night; I can't wait to meet her!'

'Oh, I'm sorry to hear that darling, you should have come and joined me in bed, I could have given you a cuddle, got you back off to sleep.' She replied. And there we were... I just didn't get adults. I've gone to her bed before in the middle of the night when I was scared once during a storm and she seemed all angry with me and sent me back to my bed, no cuddles were on offer that night! How was I to know when it was okay and not okay to go into her room?

'That's okay mum I didn't want to disturb you.' I'd learnt a long time ago that saying stuff like that made mum happy, which then in turn made my day easier. I loved my mum, and I liked to make her happy.

'Well you best get up and get ready. We don't want to be late now do we.'

'Okay mum.' I replied. 'Can I have some breakfast?'

'You're having breakfast out hun, did I forget to say that?'

'We never have breakfast out mum?' I questioned. I'm really hungry and I don't want to risk not getting anything.

'Well todays your lucky day Oli, so hurry up and get yourself ready.' She was smiling, she wasn't annoyed I was taking my time. I then wondered where I would be eating breakfast.

Half an hour later we were in mum's car and heading towards the town centre, mum seemed a little excited to me, she wasn't normally like this, ever.

'I'm going to drop you off love, and then I have some things to do in town, your Auntie said she would bring you home later when you're ready.'

'Are you not staying with us mum?' I asked, a little apprehensive about this new situation I was being launched into. She would normally stay with me the first time I met anyone new. Even family.

'You're a big boy now Oli, you don't want me cramping your style all day now do you?' She smiled; it made me feel a bit better about it all.

'What if she doesn't like me though?' I felt a bit nervous at this new freedom my mum had just given me.

'She'll love you; I can promise you that. What is there not to love about you little man!' I couldn't believe my mum, she was usually a bit over the top and protective of me, and she'd always gave me a set time I had to be home by, even when I was with my dad, but today she just seemed so chilled out about everything.

And how did she know my Auntie would love me, unless she had already met her??

We parked the car, and both got out and started walking towards McDonalds. I loved McDonalds, dad use to always take me there for my lunch if we were spending the day together, I didn't know you could have breakfast there too. Mum pushed the heavy door open and then let me walk in front of her. Mum never took me to McDonalds, I was surprised she was okay about me having my breakfast here.

'Over there.' Mum pointed towards a lady who had her back to us and was sat on her own. I looked up at my mum.

'Come on.' She took my hand like I was a little boy again and lead me over to the lady, I didn't mind though, this time.

'Hi Mia.' My mum said as we got nearer the lady. The lady turned around and look straight at me. She had tears in her eyes.

'Hello.' She said to my mum. 'Thank you so much for bringing him, this means so much to me.'

I wasn't sure what she was thanking my mum for, but my mum smiled at her, I could see mum was trying not to cry too. It was all very strange, and I didn't know what to think about it all as I'd not seem mum like this before.

'It's the least I could do Mia.' Mum said. 'You two have a lovely day now, and bring him back when you want, you've got my number if you need me for anything.'

And with that my mum gave me a kiss on the top of my head and was gone. I stood still, I think I was in shock. Shock at my mum, shock that mum and my Auntie seemed to already know each other so well, yet this was the first time I was meeting her, and shock that my Aunt really looked like my Dad, just a lady version of him.

'Hello Oliver.' She said. 'Come and sit down, and then I can go and get you something to eat if you like?' I did as she asked and went and sat opposite her. It was weird, she even sounded just like my dad too, just not so deep.

'Hello Auntie Mia.' I said as I sat down. 'It's really nice to meet you.'

'It's really nice to meet you too, Oliver. I was very happy when your mum called me, I didn't know I had a nephew, you was a nice surprise for me. I'm so sorry about your dad too Oliver. So sorry' She said. I could see it was hard for her, and she didn't even get to meet dad.

'That's okay. I've been really sad without him, and I know he would be sad I'm sad, so I try to be brave. He would be sad too that he didn't know he had a sister. You look really like him too.' I stopped there as I could see I was making her cry. I didn't want to do that as she may get angry and take me back home before we even got to do anything together.

'I'm sorry too Oliver, that I didn't get to meet him, but I'm looking forward to you telling me all about him though. ' She smiled at me, she wasn't angry at all, just sad.

'Rather than us being too sad though, why don't we get some breakfast and then we can find something fun to do for the day together?' She dried her eyes and smiled at me. 'A little birdy told me you like ice skating.'

'Thank you Auntie Mia, I'd love to do that! Can you skate? Dad could skate and he would race me around the rink.' I was beaming.

'There we go, we already have something in common, I can skate too.' She smiled and took hold of my hand. I think I am going to have a nice day with my Auntie Mia, I just wish dad had gotten to meet her too, before he died, as I think he would have liked her as much as I do. The three of us could have had lots of fun together. It was so weird, I felt like I already knew Auntie Mia, and I didn't want the day to end already.

20 YEARS LATER

T he years had flown by, I don't know where they had gone in reality. Those long lonely days that seemed to last forever a mere distance memory now. When I thought about it all it made me feel a little old, but then everyone says that don't they. It was true though. I didn't feel old with regrets about life though, I felt old having lived a very full and loved life. And today was a testament to that love.

I couldn't have felt prouder today as I stood outside the church in my beautiful dress. Mt role today was to direct people to the correct side of the church, dependant on which side of the family they came from, though I don't suppose it really mattered these days, we were all here for the same reason, the joining of two families. It was a very special role, one usually given to Paige boys, but my nephew wanted me to have this role, I think he wanted me to feel special. Everyone was here, my mother and brothers included, who all looked so proud today too. And my husband, Steven, who had been my rock, he was right by my side, proud to have me on his arm, happy to be part of this crazy family of ours. There was just one person missing today. I'd lost my father five years ago now, our differences still unresolved and taken to the grave with him. I tried not to let it get to me, some things you have no control over no matter how hard you may try. It wasn't until his passing that my brothers and

I reconnected, our fathers strong and overbearing opinion no longer a hold on them, there were free to embrace me as me. At least something positive had come out of a sad situation, and I was happy with that. I didn't hold the time lost against them; I was just glad to have them back in my life at last. Steven wasn't so forgiving of them, though he hid it well from them for me. He had his own difficult upbringing that ultimately affected the way he saw the world and how people behaved towards others. He was quite black and white about things, all things, and that was one of the many things I loved about him. He didn't think there was any excuse for my own brothers, my own flesh and blood, to have ignored me over something that wasn't my fault. He thinks they should have stood by me and loved me whatever. I often wondered on the lead up to today if my father would have put aside his prejudice's for just one day and share this experience as a united family. We'll never know that now. Maybe I wouldn't like the answer if he was here. I let the negative thoughts leave my mind. There was no place for them today, the bride had just arrived, and I want to get into the church and take me place on the front row before she made her way down the aisle towards my son.

Every family has its secrets, and there was ours, my son still thought I was his Auntie. And what a secret it was to keep from him. Everyone on our side of the family knew, they all knew my dark past as a man. The only one who didn't was my son, and the lie had gone on too long now to be able tell him otherwise. I think it would break his heart, and break his trust in me, and in his mother. None of us wanted that and as wrong as it may seem to the outside world, we had all agreed not to tell him ever. His wife to be didn't know, along with all of her family. They didn't need to know, it didn't make any difference, but it would have made a difference to my son. He'd run his Groom's speech past me the other day. He mentions me in it, Michael me that is. That was a tough one. Today he will talk about how much he still misses his dad, and how he would have loved to have shared this day with him. I don't think there will be a dry eye in the house at that point. He also thanks me, Mia me, in his speech, for the love and support and friendship I give him. I have to let him say those things, because that is how he feels. We all have such a good relationship with him, none of us want to lose him, so we will all get though his speech for him, with a few tears I'm sure, for many different reasons.

I'm sat down now, Steven's holding my hand, he knows how much today means to me, he is always there to support me, today is no different. We all stand as the bride walks in; she looks absolutely stunning. Oliver is a very lucky man, I can see he is holding back the tears as he takes in the beauty of his wife to be, and the life they have stretching ahead of them. Everything I have been fighting to hold back starts to come out, a tear of joy, pride, and sadness trickles down my face. I dab it with a hankie Steven hands me.

'No regrets' he whispers in my ear.

'No regrets' I say back to him.

ABOUT THE AUTHOR

Joseph James, the pen name of Angela Cavendish. This is Joseph James debut novel, the more thoughtful and creative side of Angela. Angela has previously had non-fiction work published, mainly articles and a book relating to horses and horse care.

Printed in Great Britain
by Amazon

22373510R00130